How Many
Miles to Babylon?

How Many Miles to Babylon?

by **Paula Fox**

AN
APPLE
PAPERBACK

SCHOLASTIC BOOK SERVICES
New York Toronto London Auckland Sydney Tokyo

ISBN 0-590-32391-1

12 11 10 9 8 7 6 5 4 3 2 1   5   2 3 4 5 6/8
Printed in the U.S.A.   11

for Richard Jackson

How many miles to Babylon?
Three score miles and ten.
Can I get there by candle-light?
Yes, and back again.

—OLD NURSERY RHYME

1

It was morning, and James Douglas awoke frightened. Perhaps it was because the light had not been turned on, and the morning city light itself was gray and cold, hardly different from early evening. Maybe it was because of the three old women, one bending over the sink, one standing against the wall opposite his bed, one sitting at the table, her head bent over an empty dish. Maybe it was because he had been thinking about how to run away from school when he went to bed the night before. Maybe it was because it was a cold November Monday in Brooklyn. He closed his eyes and pretended to sleep.

"Get up!"

"Tell him to get up!"

"Get up!"

Each one of the old women had spoken in turn. He opened his eyes and saw that the three of them had each moved to come and stand in a line beside his bed. A line of aunts; Aunt Grace who kept a towel around her head to keep off the dust, Aunt Althea who ate more than anyone else, Aunt Paul who had lost her own first name when her husband died and had taken his.

"My knee hurts," James said.

"You get up. You have to get dressed and go to school," said Aunt Grace, leaning over him. It was so dark in the room that her face was almost invisible.

"My head hurts too," he said.

"You want the police to take you to school? The principal will come in a black car to get you. *They* know you have to go to school," said Aunt Grace.

"I've got a pain in my stomach," he said.

Aunt Paul laughed.

He pushed back Aunt Grace's coat, which didn't reach far enough to cover his toes, and stood up. He had hoped they would let him stay at home so he could lie in bed and eat peanut butter on soft white bread and watch the television flicker and not think about anything. If he went to school, he might have to do something that would get him into trouble.

"Look! He slept in his underwear again!" shouted Aunt Althea. Aunt Grace shook her head. "I went to the store especially," she said. "I bought you those red pajamas so you'd like them. What's the matter with you? What would your mama think?"

"Little Bits," said Aunt Paul, for that was what she often called him, "Little Bits likes to sleep in his underwear so he'll always be ready to *go!*" She clasped his shoulder gently and shook him so that he swayed back and forth on his bare feet. The floor was cold.

"Don't call me that name," he said to Aunt Paul. The corners of her mouth turned down. She went to the straight chair near the door and sat on it. She watched him so intently while he pulled his shirt over his head, pulled up his pants, pulled on his socks, that he said, "*You're* a policeman."

"Wash!" commanded Aunt Grace. She put a little piece of white soap in his hand and hung a towel around his shoulders. He went out the door and down the long hall to the bathroom, past all the rooms where the other people lived. At night the hall was like a street because there

3

were so many people walking up and down it, shouting and knocking into each other. But now the brown doors were closed all along its length, and there wasn't any sound.

This morning, there were no surprises in the bathroom. Sometimes there were. On Friday, James had found Mr. Hedge sitting beneath the sink, his shoulders pressed up against the pipe, talking to himself. Usually Mr. Hedge was out that early, pushing his cart with his knife-sharpening wheel on it through the neighborhood and calling out — *"Knives sh-a-a-a-pon-n-ned!"* Mr. Hedge was so small he wasn't much bigger than James who was barely ten, but he had a big deep voice.

"I gotta story that'd wring your heart," he had said to James. "They broke my wheel. The man backed up his big ugly car right into my wheel. Smashed it! Smashed it to bits!" James didn't wash his hands that morning because the pipe underneath the sink leaked and it would have dripped right on Mr. Hedge.

James hadn't heard the end of Mr. Hedge's story. Still, he didn't really expect to. Stories were always beginning in his building, loud stories that filled up the halls with shouting and then fizzled out like damp firecrackers.

When he got back to the room there was a

4

bowl of cold cereal on the table. The cereal box was standing near the plate so he could read what was written on it while he ate. There was a glass of milk and a piece of bread covered with grape jelly. He poured out milk from the glass and stirred the cereal around until it looked like a pile of little brown leaves.

"He didn't wash his neck," said Aunt Althea to Aunt Grace.

"In this world if you don't wash your neck, other people will wash it for you. And your teacher will see your dirty neck and she'll think you're plain stupid!" said Aunt Grace.

"Tell me a story," James said to Aunt Paul.

She smiled instantly and sat up in the chair. "Last time I told you about the different days and what we did. Well, I didn't tell you about Wednesday morning early, did I? How we took eggs and sewed them in the hems of our dresses? Then we went to school, two miles, maybe five, and had to go early on account of the eggs was in the hems and we couldn't run to be on time. So we had to sit carefully all day until school was over and then we went to the store and traded the eggs for nice things."

"Where did you get the eggs?" James asked.

"Well . . . they was our daddy's from his hens, isn't that so, Grace? So it wasn't as if we had taken them wrongly. And we only took one or two each, enough to get a little candy or a piece of ribbon."

"Don't tell him stories about the old times," said Aunt Grace who was leaning back against the sink drinking a cup of coffee.

Aunt Althea, who was straightening his bed, turned around to say, "No. Don't tell him about all that. He's got to go to school and learn." But James wanted to hear all about that — about the country store where you could buy everything from a pork chop to a hoe, about the long dirt roads where the soft dust slipped around your bare toes, about the black stove in the kitchen where pine wood burned all winter long.

"On Mondays we washed," he began as though reciting something he had learned by heart. "On Tuesdays we ironed. On Wednesdays we scrubbed the floor with potash. On Thursdays — what did you do on Thursdays, Aunt Paul?"

"On Thursdays we went to the woods," replied Aunt Paul in a whisper, looking over at Aunt Grace who was now making the bed she shared with Aunt Althea. Aunt Grace didn't look up. Suddenly Aunt Paul said in a loud clear voice: "We went to the woods where the creek was. We found acorns and other things."

"Oh, hush!" exclaimed Aunt Grace.

"He hasn't got his books together yet," said Aunt Althea as she started to fry a few pieces of bacon on the hot plate.

James went to his bed, stooped and pulled out a cardboard box where he kept his things. His books were there, the arithmetic book and the spelling book and the reader about the dog named Spot.

"I'm going," he said.

"Eat all that lunch they give you," said Aunt Grace.

"Tell him to come straight home," said Aunt Althea.

As he closed the door, he heard Aunt Grace ask: "How did you sleep, sisters?" And Aunt Althea answered, "Not too well." Aunt Paul shouted, "I don't *have* sleep anymore. Sleep has left me."

People were beginning to wake up, all the people and dogs and cats who lived in that old building. As he walked down the stairs, he heard conversations, a few words on the fourth floor, a few more on the third and second floors, like pieces of string he could tie together. By the time he reached the sidewalk, he had one long piece of string of words: "Where did you put the . . . old window stuck . . . that I had the money in for . . . this old dog is always squeaking so leave off him Donnie . . . because she's coming today — it's the fifteenth, isn't it the fifteenth . . . when we run out of eggs."

He stood for a while in front of his building, looking at the street and the cars and the people walking or running or hobbling or moving like bits of paper in a high wind. He looked at the trash basket, a new silver one, sitting in the middle of the trash spread out all around it. He looked at two policemen walking down the middle of the street between the cars. He looked at a man with one arm who was hurrying along the curb talking to himself and waving the stump of the other arm which was hidden in his sleeve. It looked like a puppet in the puppet show James had seen at a school assembly. What was the arm saying?

A woman leaned out of a window just behind him and exclaimed, "Look at that!" in a loud voice. He wondered what she was talking about. Him?

James moved on toward the long avenue that led up to the block where his school was. He was thinking too hard to notice much, thinking about how he could get out of school once he was in it.

"Look out, boy!" said a man's voice. James

looked up at a face that stared down at him, a dark, cranky face. "Can't you see where you at?" asked the man as he walked on, clutching a big sack with newspapers sticking out of it. The man was wearing shoes that had holes cut in the tops. Maybe they weren't his shoes, thought James. He had worn someone else's shoes for a long time, shoes that Aunt Althea had brought home in her shopping bag from the place where she worked. When he had begun to walk on the sides of his feet, Aunt Paul had thrown the shoes out the back window and taken him to buy another pair of shoes. But perhaps those shoes too had belonged to somebody else. They were still too tight. He wished he had a pair of sneakers like the old woman who was just slip-slopping past him.

The one thing James was sure belonged to him was the ring he had found Saturday morning, lying on the sidewalk in front of the fried-chicken-and-ribs store.

He had picked it up and rubbed it on his jacket sleeve until the red stone glistened. It looked a little like one of the rings Aunt Paul sometimes bought for herself in the dime store. But it felt more solid. It looked real. But if it was real, how did it get there? Why hadn't someone else picked it up?

Because, he thought, it was a sign. It had been left for him by his mother, just where he would see it. He shivered at the idea of her actually standing in front of that store and leaving it for him. After Saturday he hadn't thought of anything except the ring. It meant he would have to get away from school Monday and go to the old house. And he wouldn't be able to wait until the afternoon when school was over. The ring meant he had to get there early and have plenty of time.

A dog ran to him just as he turned right, up the avenue. James didn't like dogs. They made faces at him and got in his way. There were so many of them around the place where he lived, brown and white dogs, spotted dogs, black ones with drooping tails, all running off in crooked lines through the crowds of people who walked up and down on the street, dogs that yapped and growled and knocked down the garbage cans.

Sometimes dogs followed him and he had to kick them to make them go away. This dog sniffed at his ankles. "Get away!" he cried. The dog lay down on its back, like a bug, with its legs waving right there in front of him. A woman laughed. "Looka that!" she said. The dog sprang to its feet and took off down the block. The woman walked on.

10

Had she been talking to him? James didn't like it when strangers started conversations. They often said peculiar things, then looked at him expectantly as if he was supposed to know what they were talking about.

He walked quickly. He was afraid of this street — the old brown houses were all shut up, boards nailed across the doors, windows all broken and nothing to see behind the windows except the dark rooms that always looked like night. There were piles of things on the street in front of the houses but each day there was a little less. The baby carriage he had seen last Friday was gone. The old stove was still there. Too big to carry, he guessed. Where had the people gone? One day he had seen a man up on one of the stoops kicking at the boarded-up door. "My things, my things. . . ." he had cried.

Just where James turned to get to the school street, there was an old car. Each day that he passed it, it was less of a car and more a heap of junk. Nothing was left of it now except the frame. It was terrible to look at, like a skeleton. He ran past it, then slowed to a walk. Down the block he could see all the children waiting in front of the school door. His stomach and his head and his knees really began to hurt.

He stopped where he was, hoping no one had

recognized him yet. Then he would still have a chance to turn back, to go to the old house where he had to take the ring, the place where he was completely alone, where there were things, sounds, smells that scared him and where there was something else, some feeling that made his heart thud. If he could only make up his mind!

A hand touched his shoulder and he looked up into the face of his teacher.

"Come along, James," said Miss Meadow-sweet, and James went.

2

"**J**ames Douglas! You're sleeping!" cried Miss Meadowsweet.

His hand was damp where his cheek had rested against it. For a second, he couldn't see clearly. Everyone was laughing except the teacher. "The fours," she said.

"Four times one is four," said James, still in a daze.

An eraser hit him. "Who did that?" Miss Meadowsweet shouted; the children roared.

"Four times two is eight," James said, brushing the chalk dust off his shirt.

No one heard him. Perhaps he had wakened

up into a little corner of a dream. But he saw the dark scars on his desk, the faces drawn with red ink, the carved words, the little ditch for a pencil.

Then the milk and crackers came and he didn't have to finish the fours. What were fours for? Why did he get so sleepy every morning about this time? He yawned.

"Cover your mouth with your hand when you yawn," said Miss Meadowsweet. He didn't see how she could spot him yawning in a room full of kids — dozens, fifty maybe. He didn't even know half of them. There were Buddy and Karen and Lucky who sat right near him, and a new boy in front of him who couldn't even speak English. The children called him *"Mira,"* because that's what he was always saying.

Lucky wasn't often in school because he liked to set the wastebasket on fire and he was always being sent home. Karen cried a lot. She cried when she got something wrong. She'd put her head down on her desk and say, "But I know the answer." Her notebook was full of gold stars and still she'd howl if she made just one little mistake. Buddy had used the masking tape Miss Meadowsweet kept on her desk to tape a knife to his arm. It was only a little knife but James could see where it bulged. Buddy would

say, "You do what I say, James, or I cut you!"
James didn't pay any attention because he knew
it would take Buddy too long to get the masking
tape off and get at the knife.

Then there was Ben. He was the biggest boy
in the class. He wore a blue jacket and a necktie
and he worked hard all the time. Ben never
fooled around. He was Miss Meadowsweet's
favorite — everybody knew that — but he didn't
seem to care. She smiled at him, but Ben didn't
smile at her. He just worked. At the end of the
day he put his books in his canvas bag and he
walked out of school, not looking to his left or
right. He had such a stern expression on his face
that even the older children made way for him
in the corridors, and behind his back they called
Ben "Deacon."

The Deacon was a different color from anyone
else. There were light brown children in James'
class, dark brown children like James and just a
few white children. But Ben was pale brown as
though he'd faded from some darker color, and
he had golden freckles on his nose and his hair
was reddish. James had seen him once in the
church Aunt Grace and Aunt Althea took him
to on Sunday. The church was just a little room
you walked into right off the street and the
Deacon had been sitting in the back. Right next

15

to him was a little window with colored pieces of glass stuck into it, and the light fell on the Deacon's face so that his hair looked blue and his skin red.

After church, James saw the Deacon walking away between his father and mother. They were all dressed up in clothes that looked new, not like the clothes Aunt Grace and Aunt Althea brought back from the places where they worked. Aunt Paul never brought him old things. She said he had to have his own new clothes. She said she didn't want James walking around in somebody else's old raggedy pants and Aunt Althea had called her a dreamer.

It was reading time now. James opened his book. He didn't care much about clothes; it bothered him though when the pants were too big and slid down his hips, or when the shirts smelled funny as if they had been in the bottom of some dusty old bag.

"James Douglas! Come back to us!" He jumped in his seat and fumbled for his book which fell out of his hands to the floor.

"You leave it on the floor or I fix you," whispered Buddy. James paid no attention to him. Karen reached over and showed him the place where he was supposed to read. "Look, Jane, Look!" he read. Someone had drawn a little figure wearing a tall hat falling out of the window of Jane's and Dick's house. James made a mistake.

"Not *her*, James, but *here*. Come up to the blackboard and write out both words," said Miss Meadowsweet.

When he got to the blackboard he couldn't find any chalk.

"James, go to Mr. Johnson's room and ask Mr. Johnson to give you some chalk. Politely now!" said Miss Meadowsweet.

James left his classroom feeling sleepier than ever. He must have waked up last night. He remembered now that he had seen Aunt Paul and Aunt Grace sitting in two straight chairs in front of the television set. The light from the screen had fallen on their faces and had made them look scary, like people made of wood.

What was it that had waked him? Was it Aunt Grace pointing at something he couldn't see on the screen and whispering, "Look at that! Look at the way those people behave themselves." But he was used to the Aunts whispering all night long, back and forth across the room, until the sound was like a song that rocked him back to sleep. Maybe it was the noise next door, right up against the wall where his bed was, a noise like furniture breaking.

Mr. Johnson's room was way down at the end of the corridor near the school entrance. Sometimes a policeman stood there and leaned up against the door with his hat tipped over half his face. He was a special policeman, not like the ones who directed traffic or the ones who sometimes came at night to James' building. He wore a thick black leather holster strapped to his hip. It was hard for James to imagine real feet inside the policeman's shoes.

He shivered. The policeman wasn't there today.

James felt suddenly wide awake. He hardly thought about what he was doing, but he walked right past Mr. Johnson's room and out through the front door onto the street.

The sunlight was pale yellow now, the gray clouds all swept away into one corner of the sky, like the dust Aunt Grace swept into a corner of their room every evening. He was cold but he couldn't go back to get his jacket. No, he couldn't walk into the classroom and say to Miss Meadowsweet, "I've come to get my jacket before I go." Perhaps he'd never be able to get his jacket.

Right across the street there was a row of buildings just like the one he lived in. Two yellow dogs chased a gray cat under an old black car, and all the people leaning up against the steps laughed.

What if Miss Meadowsweet came with a policeman and chased him while his three Aunts stood and watched and cried into their hands? He wouldn't be able to dive under a car like that cat. But they wouldn't find him, not where he was going. He felt in his pocket to make sure the ring was still there and then set off along the avenue.

He was a good walker. He had discovered that if he told himself stories, he could cover a lot of ground without noticing how much time it took. Once last year, all the subways in New York had stopped running because the men who ran the trains went on strike, and Aunt Paul had had to walk miles because the lady she worked for every day wouldn't pay her wages if she didn't show up. The subway workers wanted more money. That was easy for James to understand; everybody he knew wanted more money.

James' school was closed during the strike because the teachers couldn't get to it. So he and Aunt Paul had left early one morning, when the sun was barely up, and they had walked toward Flatbush Avenue with hundreds of people. When they finally got to the big apartment house where she worked, Aunt Paul said that

she was just sick and hardly knew how she'd get
through the day thinking about walking all the
way back home. For the first time he could
remember, Aunt Paul had been cross with him.
She had told him to sit down on a chair in the
lady's kitchen and *not move* until she said he
could.

Walking away from school now, looking at his
feet as they moved, first one, then the other, he
told himself the story of that day. He had sat in
the kitchen with all those green plants lined up
on the window sill and looked at everything
until the toaster and the coffee pot and all the
pots and pans and the stove became one big
silver blur. Then Aunt Paul had come in and
said the Missus had gone out and he could look
at the other rooms. The whole place was like a
big store except that there were no price tags on
anything. All the time he was looking, his Aunt
Paul was wiping furniture or running the
vacuum cleaner, or carrying a pail of water and
a mop somewhere.

She had told him not to touch anything, but he
did. He touched two white keys on the piano and
he picked up a little carved sheep made out of
some kind of white stone. The sheep had a bell
that really rang tied around its neck. James
wanted to put it in his pocket and take it home.

Aunt Paul told him to put it right down. "She's very particular about her things," she had said. "If she catch you playing with that, I don't know what she'd do!"

Right inside that apartment there were two bathrooms, and so many closed doors he wondered if other families lived there. But most of the doors led to closets. "You can go into the boy's room," his Aunt had said, "but you stand right in the middle of the floor and don't hardly move."

The boy's room had shelves of toys and other shelves of books and a bicycle with its own stand in a corner. He couldn't bear that room, not while he had to be so still in the middle of the floor.

He had a piece of chocolate cake after his lunch. "Don't try to get it all in your mouth at once, Little Bits. There's plenty more," Aunt Paul had said.

Later that day the lady came back. She had on gloves and she patted his head. "Well . . . so this is *her* son," the lady had said to Aunt Paul. "Yes, ma'am. That's him," Aunt Paul had said. "Nice-looking," said the lady and she took a bunch of flowers from a vase and gave them to Aunt Paul. "You might catch a ride," she said. "I saw a lot of trucks stopping for people. Isn't it awful how this strike can tie up the whole city?" "Yes, ma'am," said Aunt Paul.

Aunt Paul filled her shopping bag with other paper bags and some balls of string, and she stuck the flowers in on top. Then they went down to the wide street which ran along beside a big park. They caught a ride too. A big truck with canvas flaps at the back stopped for them, and a lot of arms reached out and pulled them both in behind the flaps. James was so tired he had leaned against his Aunt. "That's where your mother worked before she got sick and had to go to the hospital," she said. The words woke him up. His mother had been in that same place and had known all about the bicycle and the little stone sheep with the bell. He sat in the dark thinking about those rooms with his mother walking through them, wondering why she had never told him about it, and smelling the funny sour smell of the flowers the lady had given Aunt Paul.

James had told himself the story of that day many times and each time he was able to remember more clearly what things had felt like and tasted like, how they had looked. It was the same with all the stories he told himself — whether they had really happened or not, they seemed to get clearer as he thought about them.

James looked up.

He had come to the street which his Aunts had told him never to cross. It was a different part of town, they said. On the other side of the street were little apartment houses, light brown, with curtains in the windows and little skinny black fire escapes zig-zagging down to the street. Last time he had been here, he had seen some children his own age playing ball on the sidewalk. Some of them had hair the color of margarine. Aunt Paul had said that this was the kind of place she'd like to live in, and Aunt Althea had laughed and declared that Aunt Paul's mind was leaving her.

He turned right and walked two blocks and then right again and there was the empty house. James had found it almost a month ago, right after his birthday and two months after his mother had gone away. It was a real house made of wood with a sagging wooden porch and a doorbell hanging out on its wire near the door. It had a peaked roof and most of the windows were broken. There was a little rusty fence like a line of written "m's" all around the front, and a soft old black tire inside where there were little tufts of yellowed grass.

Before he took a step on the path, James

looked up and down the street. A woman was pushing a baby carriage around the corner. The two gray buildings on either side of the house showed no sign of life. Nobody leaned out of the windows like people did in his building. Across the street was a place where you took laundry. He could see some women sitting in front of the washing machines looking at magazines. The only living thing on the street at the moment was a little brown dog tied up to a bus-stop sign by a long rope. The dog watched him silently.

James wished the dog was not looking at him. He didn't want to be seen going into the house, even by a dog. He *knew* he shouldn't go into the house — it wasn't his house. But that wasn't the reason why he wanted the street to be empty when he walked up the little path. What he knew and what he felt were two different things. He felt that going into that house had to be something he did secretly, as though it were night and he moved among shadows.

The door was open enough to let him slip in without pushing it. Sunlight didn't penetrate the dirty windows, so he stood still until his eyes grew accustomed to the darkness. Then, as he smelled the dusty old rooms and the dampness of the wallpaper that was peeling off the walls, other things he felt came swimming toward him through the gloom like fish.

James knew that his mother had gotten so sick one night that she had had to go away to a hospital. He knew that she couldn't write to him because she had to wait until she got better before she could do anything except lie flat and still. Sometimes Aunt Grace got a letter from the hospital telling how she was coming along. He knew that he had once lived in another room where there had been only three people, his father, his mother and himself, and that his father was mostly home and his mother was out working, and that one night the light which had hung from the middle of the ceiling, like the light in his Aunt's room, had never gone out. His mother had spent that night standing next to the window looking into the street. After that he had not seen his father again, and when he asked his mother about him she had said, "Gone, gone, gone. . . ." just like that, three times. Then they had moved in with the three Aunts, who were not really his Aunts but his father's. That same day someone had given him a bag of jelly beans.

That was the story of what had happened. But James had discovered another story hidden just beneath it. It was different from the first, but if he felt it, wasn't it true? When his Aunts talked about his mother being in the hospital, he wanted to tell them she was in Africa. Yet when he was walking along somewhere, thinking, or sitting at his desk in school, picturing her there in Africa, something in *him* said, no, she was sick and in the hospital. It was like having his arms yanked by two people going in different directions. But when he came to this house, the stories came together and were one.

Then James knew and felt the same thing! He was being guarded by those three old women so that no harm would come to him. His mother had gone across the ocean to their real country, and until she came back, no one was supposed to know who he really was. She had to fix everything. She had to see the people who lived in the deserts and the mountains, in the forests and the cities and tell them about him. But he knew he was not the only prince. He knew there were others. When everything was all right, all the princes would come together in a great clearing dressed in their long bright robes and their feathers, and after that everything would be different.

James knew how a prince would dress. He had seen pictures of princes and the villages they lived in. He had seen them dance on television and in the movies, but his mother had told him how the real life of all those princes had come to an end long ago, how they had been made to march for days and weeks through the wild forests, with their hands chained and their necks in ropes, until they came to a river where they were put in boats which carried them across the water.

Even though James had a good memory, he couldn't recall his mother ever telling him any other story except that one. She didn't talk much. But sitting there one morning across the table from him she had just begun, even though he wasn't looking at her. It was pouring rain outside and they were alone in the room. "What happened then?" he had asked her, because he was so afraid she would stop and not say any more, just get quiet the way she usually was and watch him and not speak. But she had gone on. She said that all those people would never recognize each other again, and no one knew who his own grandparents were.

But his mother must have found a secret paper that told all about James' great-great-great-grandfather who had been a king. She had left the ring for him so that he would know how hard she was working to make everything fine.

"King," he whispered to himself as he felt his

way down the stairs to the basement. The word gave him courage. He hadn't gotten used to that basement yet, and some of the things he *knew* scared him: rats cannonballing out of corners, fanged like snakes, damp and gray; or the people who really owned the house suddenly coming back and finding him there, tying him up and sending him away to jail.

The basement was very cold. He fumbled around in the dark until his knees bumped up against the orange crate, then he reached in his pocket and took out a book of matches. He lit one and saw the soup can with the candle stub stuck in it. There was a strong draft blowing through the basement, so he had to light a lot of matches before he got the candle lit.

Great shadows swelled and sprang at the walls or shrank into dense black pools on the floor. James opened the box next to the can and took out the things he needed. There were some feathers from a duster, a little bottle of white paste and tubes and little jars of paint, blue and red and gray and white, that Aunt Althea had brought home one day in her shopping bag. There was a piece of red curtain he had found upstairs and a band with some feathers pasted on it and a pair of old slippers that Aunt Paul had thrown away.

When he had first come to the house, he had been able to go barefoot. But now it was too cold and the floor felt wet as though water had leaked in from the ground. The only sound he heard was the little noise he made opening jars. He began to paint his face, a line down his nose, across his forehead, slanting across his cheeks, but he didn't use very much because later he would have to rub it all off on the red curtain so that his Aunts wouldn't find a trace of it. Then he tied the band around his head, and the feathers hung down and tickled his cheeks. He stopped his work for a minute and ate a cheese cracker he found in his pocket. He wasn't scared now. He had even begun to feel quite warm. He tied the curtain around himself, making a big knot around his neck from two of the ends and pulling the other two in at his waist with a rope he'd found in the bathroom one morning. He took off his shoes and slid his feet into the slippers. Then, his heart beating faster, he took candle and ring and walked back to the other end of the basement.

The flicker of light showed him first the giant black boots, then the huge red-clothed legs, then the black belt with the silver buckle, then the white beard almost covering the face, the two apple cheeks, the small gleaming eyes, then the cap with the bell disappearing into the darkness above. He held the candle up high until he could see the whole giant cardboard figure, three times taller than he was, leaning up against the wall, the eyes staring straight ahead.

He put the candle down, placed the ring in front of the figure and clapped his hands softly, then harder. James began to dance, hopping on one foot and then the other, brushing his slippered feet on the floor, bending back and forward as far as he could. He never quite took his glance from the bright eyes of the figure. If the dance was right, those eyes would see him, recognize him, and his mother would know he had found the ring. Slowly his clapping grew louder; he bent and whirled until it seemed to him he was dancing before an immense fire that warmed and comforted him.

Then just when James thought the eyes had found him at last, he heard such a shriek that he spun on his heels and leapt back until he had fallen against the figure, his arms flung out, the feathered band falling over his face.

There was a second shriek, then shouts, and James realized that what he had heard was laughter.

"Look at — look at!" said a voice. "We got a Sandy Claus in our house!"

"Yeah. He got his dwarf with him too," said a second.

"Sandy Claus and his dwarf," said the first.

Two figures emerged from the darkness. One was tall and skinny and had a black cloth wrapped around his head. One earring gleamed in his ear. The other was short and plump and carried a torn umbrella, one of its metal ribs sticking straight out.

"Well, well, you never know, do you, Blue?" said the tall skinny one.

"No, Stick, you never do know."

"Can I go?" cried James, his voice trembling.

"The dwarf speaks English. Here I thought it'd speak Sandy Claus," said Stick.

"Yeah. That's just what I thought. Say a word in Sandy Claus, dwarf," said Blue.

"Please. Can I go?" pleaded James.

They stared down at him. They weren't so much bigger than he was after all, but big enough. Stick turned his head toward Blue.

"I just got an idea," said Stick. "We can use him to get the dogs."

"A whole idea?" said Blue. "You improving."

"We could use us a dwarf," said Stick, grinning.

"What's your name, dwarf?" asked Blue.

Thinking suddenly of his mother, her black hair tumbling down her back, dressed in a long white gown, stronger than anyone, thinking of the big clearing where all the people would come together, of the princes who would be there, James darted forward and picked up the ring. He held it out above the candle so they could see it. For a second he forgot what he knew, and only said what he felt.

"I'm a prince," he cried.

The two of them threw back their heads and shouted with laughter. They clutched themselves around their middles and staggered and stamped on the floor with their feet.

"A prince!" howled Blue.

"Yeah. A little black prince," yelled Stick. "Wait'll Gino hear this." Then they both stopped laughing at the same moment and Stick reached out and grabbed the ring from James' hand.

"Look here, he got himself a ring from a candy box. A ring for a black prince," said Stick.

"Let's see that valuable ring. Look at that! They let us in the subway for free if we flash this ring," said Blue. Then he threw the ring into the farthest corner of the basement.

James tore off the red curtain and ran for the stairs, but the big slippers tripped him up and Stick caught hold of his arm.

"No, no, Prince," said Blue. "You going to stay with us. We got work for you to do. If you be good, maybe we'll make you a king. We got the power, Prince. If you don't be good, we keep you a dwarf."

"Go get Gino," said Stick. "We got to change our plan."

3

What scared James about Gino was his size. Gino was no taller than James was himself, yet he looked so old. His voice was unlike any voice James had ever heard. Every time Gino spoke it was as if a door with a rusty hinge was swinging in the wind.

Gino stared at James as though he were a bug. James looked at Gino's hands which were balled into fists. Even by the dim light of the candle, he could see the dark hair curling on the pale skin of Gino's fingers.

"We could use him," Blue said.

"What for? What you got in your head?" Gino

replied. "How do we know what he's up to?"

"I got an idea about him," said Stick, jabbing James' neck with his finger. "If this dwarf go up to somebody's door and ring the bell, they not going to think anything about letting him take their dog, right? He look all sweet and cool."

Gino pinched his nose and shook his head.

"What if he say something to the people while he's getting the dog — like he might tell them about us?" he said finally.

"He's not going to say nothing to nobody because he going to know Stick and Blue and Gino is right near by, waiting," Stick said.

"He could run into the house and close the door. Then how could we get at him?" Gino asked.

"Naw!" exclaimed Blue. "You think the people going to let him in? If he jump at the door, the people going to push him out. What do it matter what he say? You know they're not going to believe him. But we'll know if he say something. And we'll bring him back to this old house and we let old Sandy Claus swallow him up."

James had been taking small steps backward while they talked. Only one more! But he was so scared —

"And if the people call the cops," Stick was

saying, "so what? We be gone by that time and all they got is this little bitty kid. The cops going to think he's crazy. They'll lock him up!"

James reached out behind him. It was like being on the edge of a cliff. If he didn't make it, he'd fall into a bottomless hole. But they weren't looking at him now. All three of them had their hands in their pockets. They were staring down at the floor.

His arms held out like a bird's wings, his head down like a ram, James whirled and flung himself at the stairs. He scrambled up three steps before they caught hold of his legs, and dragged him back down.

"Now, look at that!" Blue said. "He don't like our company!"

"He's not reliable," said Gino.

Stick laughed.

Blue said to James, "Rub that paint off your face. Put on your shoes. We can't carry you around with those trashy old slippers."

While the three of them watched, James wiped his face on the curtain, then put on his shoes. His fingers trembled so he couldn't tie the double knot Aunt Paul had taught him how to make.

"Listen!" Stick's voice rattled close to James' ear.

Blue said, "Prince, he said *listen!*"

How could he listen? They sounded like three radios going at once.

"You going to help us," Stick said. He was squatting down next to James. "We're going to take you to these apartment houses and you going to go inside. Then you going to somebody's door and ring the bell. When the door opens, you say, 'Ma'am, you got a dog you want me to walk?'"

"Yes, little child, I got a dog," Blue said in a lady's high thin voice. "She weigh three hundred pounds and she love little boys —"

"Blue, I'll break your head, you don't shut up," Stick said.

James stood up. His legs ached from squatting. Stick rose swiftly at the same time. "You smile nice when you ask for the dog," he said.

"Listen, dwarf," said Blue. "Maybe you shiver a little so she see how cold you are."

"If they got no dog," Gino said, "you just go. If she got a great big dog, you say, 'No ma'am, he's too big for me to take care of.' The dog you get has to fit into a little box, see? Now, if she say no, the dog been out already, you say you can come back later. But if she say okay, you say you charge a dime."

"Don't you ask for no fifteen cents," Stick said.

Gino took hold of James' arm. Even though Gino's fingers were wrapped tightly around it,

James could feel Gino moving away as if he hated to touch him. "You got to remember the most important thing," Gino said. "You don't say one more word than what I explained. *Not one more word.*"

"Then you bring us the dog," Stick said.

"Get your coat," Blue said to James.

"I don't have a coat," James said instantly, almost grateful that one of them had said something he could understand.

Gino moaned and let go of James' arm. "He don't even have a coat," he said. "I changed my mind. How we going to take him like that? People going to look at him, and they're going to look at us. Then a cop car's going to stop — "

Stick interrupted: "Nobody going to bother about him. What they care if he got a coat or not got a coat?"

Meanwhile Blue had unwound a long brown scarf from his neck. He wound it around James' shoulders, around and around until only James' eyes were clear of the musty, prickly wool.

"Looks funny," said Gino.

"Looks like a little old shrunk-up man," said Stick.

"How we going to carry him?" asked Gino.

"You seen that tire out in front of the house?" Stick asked Blue.

"Yeah, I seen it," answered Blue.

"Go get it," said Stick.

Blue disappeared up the stairs. Gino shook his head.

"We ought to tie him up and leave him here. Maybe he'll write a note to somebody."

"Can you write?" Stick asked, grabbing James' shoulder.

James supposed it would be best to say that he couldn't. He guessed he should say no to all their questions. Yet he couldn't help saying, "I can write."

"What'd he say?" asked Gino, scowling.

"Take the blanket off your mouth and speak up," said Stick.

Blue came back then, holding the tire in his hands. Stick motioned James up the stairs. "I got to have more light," he said to Gino.

All the time that Stick was standing near a window at the back of the big room on the first floor and cutting up the tire into equal lengths, Gino held onto James' arm. James stared at the knife in Stick's hands, seeing how it flew back and forth carving the rubber, whacking off a piece here, a piece there, trimming and scraping.

James felt tears in his eyes. He closed them

hard and told himself he must not cry. He must not!

Now Stick reached into a pocket and took out a handful of string. He tied up the tire sections.

"A saddle," he said.

"Ride 'em, cowboy!" said Blue.

"Shut up!" said Gino.

"He's gonna ride with you, Gino. Blue too fat and I'm too thin. You're just right," Stick said. "Gino and his dwarf. That make two dwarfs."

Gino looked at Stick, then at Blue. His fingers crawled off James' arm. He seemed to be blowing up like a balloon, yet staying his own size. He didn't say a word, just moved his head from side to side. A broken tooth gleamed in his mouth. James backed toward the door. No one appeared to notice. He kept backing up.

Then Stick whispered, "Don't move, Prince."

James stood still. He could hear Blue wheezing. Stick gulped. James looked frantically at the front door. He'd never make it. He'd run into Stick's knife before he took two steps. Then Gino opened his mouth wide and snorted with laughter. Stick and Blue laughed. They stamped on the floor. Blue was circling, circling, snapping his fingers. The dust rose until the air seemed full of gray fuzz. Stick shut the blade of his knife and stuck it back in his pocket.

"Let's go," he said.

Gino went first, after glancing out at the street through the front window. He beckoned. Stick and Blue each took one of James' arms.

"Clear," whispered Gino.

They walked out on the porch, down the steps and around to the side of the house where three bicycles had been left leaning up against the wall. Each bike had a wooden box strapped to it. Stick began to tie the tire sections onto the back wheel of one of the bikes. Gino peered into one of the boxes. "You didn't get enough dog food," he said to Blue.

"Whaddya mean, I didn't get enough? You must be thinking we got elephants to feed."

"We can get more," Stick said. "We got to get out of here now. We got a lot of traveling to do." Then he said to Gino, "Four rooms upstairs. Plenty of room, if we're going to use this house instead of Coney. Maybe we could get us four dogs today."

James didn't know what they were talking about. His arms were cold. He tried getting the scarf over them but then it pulled away from his neck.

"Leave that rag around your neck," Stick said. "You going to be colder when we riding."

"Can I go back and get my ring?" asked

James, his voice trembling slightly. If he could have the ring in his pocket, he wouldn't feel so terrible.

"No, you can't get nothing," said Gino.

James looked down at the ground. It was hard under his feet and the earth was gray. The grass was dead. He made up his mind there and then that he would not beg them for anything.

"Don't you bring us no yippers," Gino said. "None of them yapping little dogs. You understand?"

"Gino, whyn't you shut up and stop your worrying?" asked Stick. Gino scowled and kicked the ground.

"If you be good," Blue said to James, "we'll get you some dwarf food later."

"And if you be bad —" Stick said, but he didn't finish.

Gino started to mount his bike. Stick held up his hand and James saw how thin his wrist was. He noticed Stick was wearing a big watch, but the watch had no hands on it. Gino suddenly turned around. "What if somebody ask why he out of school?" he asked.

"I thought of that," Stick said. He looked at James. "Listen! Anyone ask you why you not in school, you say you go in the morning. You say your school get too many kids so some have to go in the morning and some have to go in the afternoon."

James felt dizzy. He wished he could make a story out of what was happening to him right now — pretend he was just walking home to his Aunts, to his bed in the corner. . . . What were they going to do with those dogs they were talking about? James didn't just dislike dogs. He was a little afraid of them.

"Let's go, Stick," Blue said. "Dog business incorporated got to get on the road."

Stick shoved James over toward Gino's bike. "All right," he said. "Everybody up!"

James got himself up on the back wheel and grabbed Gino. Beneath the chilled leather of Gino's jacket, James could feel how little he was, but hard and bony. He would rather have ridden behind Blue, even Stick.

Blue led the way, half-walking, half-wheeling his bike around the corner of the house. "All clear," he called back.

The street looked the same as it had to James — how long ago? He couldn't even guess. It might have been hours since he had gone into the old house. It might have been days that he had known Gino and Stick and Blue.

If only he hadn't found that ring! Then he would not have left school. Even if he could get away from Gino, even if he could get home to his Aunts, he was in serious trouble. The ring! In his pocket, it was magic, but lying in a dusty corner, it was just what Stick had called it, a candy-box ring, good for nothing.

Oh — but his mother! If she knew — if she could see what was happening to him! She would take Stick and Blue and Gino and put them in a sack and drop them off a building. Then he and she would get into her long, black car and — "You squeezing me to death!" shouted Gino, his voice grating like a bottle top on pavement, the words soon lost among the cars and buses and trucks. The bike knifed its way through the traffic with abrupt turns right and left, plunging down streets where people stood in clumps around the lamp posts, their faces turned toward the street, looking but not seeing James, just as if nothing extraordinary was happening to him. No one knew he was stuck to Gino as if he'd been glued to him. If he let go, he'd fall on the pavement beneath. If he called out, no one would hear him. The wind would take his voice and carry it away. And he was freezing. His neck and chin were warm, but his arms felt as though they were turning to stone. He dug his head into Gino's jacket.

Horns honked wildly. Gino came to a sudden

stop near a traffic light. James reeled forward.
Blue had run into a heap of empty garbage cans
and the lids were rolling all over the street. Blue
was hopping around, grabbing up the lids from
in front of the cars and tossing them back on the
sidewalk while angry drivers shouted at him
from their cars. Stick had stopped a few feet
away and was balancing himself with one foot
on the curb. He was staring at Blue as if he'd
never seen anything so peculiar in his life. Gino
was muttering to himself.

A group of children were walking toward
Blue. James looked around. He saw that he was
within a block of his school, and those children
were the ones who went home for lunch. One of
them, taller than the others, walking off by
himself, was the Deacon.

Gino's foot came down hard on the pedal and
they were off, Blue riding behind Stick and
Stick just a wheel away from Gino. As they
began gathering speed, the Deacon looked up
and for an instant his eyes met James' eyes. For
the first time that day, James laughed. He had
never seen anyone look so surprised. The Deacon's mouth opened; his eyes widened; he
dropped his fine briefcase. Then he pivoted on
his heel, looking after the three bike riders as
they sped down the avenue. James, turning

back to Gino's jacket, kept on laughing. He would have waved if he had dared to let go.

A second later, he wondered how he could have laughed at all. Gino and the other two had speeded up, and Gino was leaning so far forward over the handlebars that James felt he was only hanging on to the air itself. The bikes slowed again. Gino's back seemed to pull farther and farther away as though every bit of him hated James.

"Lemme go," said Gino. James slid off the tire.

"Who was you laughing at?" Stick asked James angrily.

"Dwarfs not allowed to laugh," Blue said.

"I saw you laughing. I saw that kid looking at you back there like he knew you," Stick said, at the same time taking one of James' ears between two of his fingers and, very gently, exerting pressure.

"Now we're through!" Gino cried. "Someone seen him and us! See what I told you?"

The pressure on James' ear increased. Suddenly there was no more pressure. The ground gave way beneath his feet. He was turned upside down and all he could see were feet, and legs that shivered with cold, and bicycle wheels. Stick was holding him up by his ankles and swinging him back and forth. The sky was coming down on him.

"Boy!" called Stick over James' feet. "Did you know that kid that looked at you so hard?"

"No!" cried James, his voice falling back into his throat. He cried again, "No! I didn't know him!" Slowly the ground came back and the sky drifted away and he was on his feet.

"Then what was you laughing at?" Stick asked in an everyday voice.

"I laughed because of the garbage cans. That's why I laughed," James said, gulping as if his lies were pieces of hard candy too big to swallow.

Stick leaned against the wall and stared at James. He didn't scowl or smile. He looked like a stone. Gino creaked. James saw that he was laughing, only instead of *ha-ha* all Gino could do was make that rusty sound.

"Okay, Prince," Stick said suddenly as if he had made up his mind.

They hadn't known what he had been laughing about, James realized. They couldn't tell what he was really *thinking*. They could make him go where they wanted and they could scare him. But they couldn't get inside his head where his thoughts were. Maybe he'd have a great thought that would show him how he could get home.

47

4

"We'll try that apartment house there," Stick said, pointing to a large building across the street from the park. "You tell the doorman your mother work upstairs. Tell him — " Stick looked up, counting the floors — "Say she in apartment 11-G. What's the matter with you?"

James felt wild. His mother! Maybe it was true, that she was really up there in that apartment, 11-G.

"Nothing," he said.

Blue said, "His mama don't work, carrying no buckets around. You crazy, Stick? A prince's mama don't work. She just stay home and polish up the crowns."

Stick ignored Blue. "You tell the doorman over there that you got a message from home. Tell him your daddy is sick. You got it? But don't say nothing if he don't ask you nothing."

James nodded and started off to cross the street.

"Wait for the light," Blue called out. James turned back to look at him. Blue had sounded like one of James' Aunts, worrying about cars. Blue was grinning, as usual.

"Wrap up that scarf," Gino called out crossly. "You look nuts with it hanging around you like that."

James wound the scarf around his throat. He walked across the street. The doorman was talking to another man. Just as James reached the sidewalk, the doorman held a little radio up to his ear. Then both men saw James at the same time.

"Look at that!" exclaimed the doorman.

"Yeah. . . . Why are you wearing that blanket, kid?" asked the second.

"You can't never tell what they are up to," muttered the doorman.

"My mother . . . I got to see her. She's up in 11-C," said James, not daring to look directly at the men. He had already gotten the apartment number wrong. He'd heard 11-C come right out of his mouth even though he'd meant to say 11-G.

"Your mother? Hmm . . ." the doorman said. He pushed in the antenna of his radio. "That's pretty funny. Because 11-C is an empty. It's for rent, see? So if your mother's up there, what I got to ask you is what she doing up there? Hunh? Or are you thinking of renting the apartment? Whaddya say?"

Suddenly frantic, suddenly feeling his mother really was somewhere in the building waiting for him, James spoke so quickly his words tumbled out of his mouth. "Maybe I got the number wrong, but I know she's up there. I'd know the door. I came with her once."

The doorman tipped his hat back. "All right, kid," he said, as if he were giving James the building. "You can go up. But you come right down if you don't find her. No hanging around in my apartment house." The doorman and the other man walked away and left James standing at the entrance to the lobby. He saw the doorman pull up the radio antenna.

The lobby was like a tunnel — cool, dark, drafty. In front of him was a door with a round window at the top and above it a kind of clock

50

with one hand. He pressed the red button next to the door and it slid back soundlessly. Inside the elevator, he pressed a button marked 11. The elevator moved upward slowly while James stared at himself in a little mirror hanging from one corner. It made him look old, shrunken. Maybe he was a dwarf. He felt now the way he had when he'd gone to the hospital where he and Aunt Grace had waited all morning in a big room full of hard yellow benches until the doctor had called him to look at his sore throat. He felt the way he had when he saw the hypodermic needle in the doctor's hand and knew it was going to go into his arm and that it was going to hurt. There hadn't been a thing he could do to stop that needle. There wasn't a thing he could do now to get away from Gino and Blue and Stick. He'd run away from school. He'd lied about the Deacon. He'd lied to the doorman. And those three were waiting for him down there on the sidewalk. There wasn't a thing he could do.

The elevator came to a stop and the door slid back. The hall had green walls. There was a little light in the ceiling. The doors were all closed. It looked like a cemetery. There was a newspaper on one doormat. He pushed open a gray metal door which didn't have a doorknob,

51

at one end of the hall. He saw garbage cans, some faded flowers wrapped in a piece of tissue paper, and a quart of milk by another door. He realized how hungry he was. Everybody in school would have had lunch by now. The Deacon would be walking back to class, carrying his briefcase, not looking right or left or talking to anyone, his stomach full of food. James wished he were the Deacon. He was sure the Deacon would never have gotten himself into this kind of mess.

He went back to the hall and looked at each door. The longer he waited to ring a bell, the more scared he got. What would happen if he stayed up on the eleventh floor and waited until dark, then tried to find his way home? No. Gino would wait even if the others gave up. And the doorman would come looking for him.

He took a long step forward and pressed his finger against the bell of the door in front of him. A voice called out, "Who's there?"

James trembled. Surely she'd know his voice!

"I said, who's there?"

"Me," he said. But he knew how silly his answer was, just as he knew at that same moment that there was a stranger on the other side of the door.

There was a long pause, then the door opened

a crack and he saw a strip of face peering down at him. A chain was unhooked and the door opened.

"Well!" said the woman. She had yellow hair and it was springing up all over her head like feathers flying out of a pillow. She was wearing a long dress with feathers around the neck so that she looked to James like a big yellow chicken. She clucked at him.

"Miss. You got a dog?" he asked.

She glanced hurriedly over her shoulder. "No!" she whispered, as though she were afraid someone was listening. "I've got a cat, a great big awful cat that's ruining my silk upholstery. If my cat saw a dog — where *is* the dog? Didn't you say you found a dog? If my cat saw a dog, he'd roll it all up into a little ball and *swallow* it!" She scowled. "Where's that dog?" she asked again.

"I haven't got a dog," James said. The woman shrugged her shoulders.

"Things get funnier all the time," she said, hooked the chain, clucked once more and closed the door.

Left alone again in the hall, James discovered he was less frightened than he had been. He rang another bell. Instantly there was a bark, then another, then a whole series and the sound of a dog sniffing at the bottom of the door.

"Hush, Gladys!" said someone. The door opened wide. A small white fuzzy dog shot out into the hall as if she'd been hurled from a rubber band and flung herself at James' knees. She licked his hand with a pink tongue.

"Gladys!" said the woman standing there. "Behave!"

"You got a dog?" asked James, then looked down at his feet where Gladys was now lying on her back, wriggling.

The woman laughed. "Some people think Gladys is a dog," she said.

"Well — you want me to take her for a walk?" asked James. "Ten cents," he added.

"Is that your business, dog-walking?" asked the woman.

"Yes, ma'am," James replied.

"Shouldn't you be in school?"

"I don't go until later," he said. "The schools are so crowded they've got to have half the classes in the morning and half in the afternoon."

"Well, you're an enterprising boy," said the woman. "Just a minute," she added. Gladys scrambled up and raced after her as she went back down her hall. The door slammed shut. James didn't know what to do. He had just decided that he'd have to try another door when the lady appeared again with Gladys leaping on the end of a red leash like a hooked fish. The woman held out her hand. In it was a cookie. As he took it, James rested his hand in hers for a second. It was a warm hand. He wished he could crawl into it. "Thanks," he said.

She smiled. "All right. You certainly are enterprising. Gladys likes the park, just inside the entrance before you get to the playground."

He nodded, then Gladys and he were alone in the hall. She was panting and making dog faces at him, but she didn't bother him the way dogs usually did. Perhaps it was because she was so small. She sat down in the elevator and looked up at him. He noticed that she had a red ribbon tied around the tuft of fur on her head.

"You're going for a ride, not a walk," James said to her.

When he got to the lobby, the doorman was leaning against the wall reading a newspaper.

Now what should he do? It wasn't so hard to think of what *he* could say, but it was hard to think of what the doorman would say. James tiptoed past him but Gladys' black claws sounded like a box of tacks spilling on the floor.

The doorman dropped the newspaper.

"Whoa! Where are you going with that dog?" he cried.

"A lady asked me to take her out," said James.

"You just stand right there," said the door-man. He walked over to a black panel covered with buttons, pressed one and picked up a phone.

"Oh, Mrs. Flinch? It's just me, Al. Say, did you ask a little kid to take out Gladys?" The doorman listened, then nodded as though Mrs. Flinch could see him. Then he put back the receiver and nodded at James. "Okay," he said.

James walked down to the corner aware of a flash of metal across the street as three bicycles were wheeled along keeping pace with him. He crossed over. He was about to tell Blue what had happened when Stick whispered ferociously, "Keep walking. Don't look at us. Go into the park. Keep out of sight. Don't walk so fast. Stop looking back. Keep your head up. Don't drag the dog."

James turned in at the park entrance, trying to keep Gladys from frisking right off the leash. Stick came over to him.

"Pretty good," he said. "A poodle. Now walk down behind that rock and wait there until we come."

The path sloped down a small incline, wound around a pond and disappeared behind a large rock. A few yards beyond the rock there ran a wide road on which, at that moment, a horde of cars came to a stop. James was sure everybody was looking at him, suspecting him. It was a good thing dogs couldn't talk — or wouldn't, he thought.

What were they going to do to Gladys? James began to feel bad about her. He was surprised at himself. With what he had on his mind why should he fuss about a dog? Yet he was fussing, scared for her, thinking maybe he'd just let her loose and tell *them* she'd gotten away. His hand went out to Gladys' collar, hesitated, petted her instead of unleashing her. Well — she was all right for a dog . . . but they'd *kill* him this time if he did anything wrong. He straightened up to see Stick waiting beside the rock. James watched the way he stood so quietly, no expression on his face at all. The cars snorted and rushed on down the road. It was hard, thought James, not to be scared. But it was even harder to say something when you were.

"What are you going to do with this dog?" he asked. His voice rose at the end of his sentence as though he were going to cry. He was angry with himself.

Stick looked at him, his face frozen. "We're going to do what we're going to do," he said in a low awful voice. Then Blue came around the rock with Gino just behind him. "Now, Stick, you acting like the big man! Go on . . . tell him," said Blue in a teasing, laughing way. "I'll tell him. He's going to have to help us anyhow."

"Shut your face," Stick said in the same voice.

But Blue went on talking. "We keep the dogs," he said, "and we buy a newspaper a couple of days from now. They got a special part of the paper — lost and found. If people care about their dog, the put an ad in there and it say *reward.* Then Gino take the dog back and collect the reward and then we share it. The reason Gino he do it is because the people don't suspect him like they do us. Now, what you think, Prince? That idea took brains, didn't it? *My* brains! My idea! — " Stick brought his hand around so fast that James didn't see it until it slammed Blue's chin. At the sound of the slap, James ducked.

Gladys barked and stood up at the end of her leash. Gino looked down at his feet, his shoulders all hunched up. Blue was suddenly sitting on the ground, his head bent over as though he were watching a crawling ant.

"Didn't I say not to tell him?" asked Stick softly. "I don't care if it was your idea. It belongs to *me* now! Me and Gino."

James yanked on the leash. His feet were out

58

of control. They carried him along to the road all the time his head was telling him: Go back! Go back! They'll do something terrible to you now! But his feet didn't listen, carrying him right out on the road where drivers shouted at him as they whirled by. Could he make it now? He didn't dare take the time to look back. Gladys was pulling him along, the leash pinching his fingers as he tried to untangle his hand.

Gino caught up with him just as he had gained the path on the other side of the road. James began to cry. Gino took hold of his arm and dragged him back to Stick. Blue was standing up now and leaning against the rock. He was rubbing his chin.

"Don't cry," said Blue to James. "When you cry, everybody else laugh."

James wiped his eyes with one hand. Gino let go of his arm. Then he stooped a little so his face was right next to James'. "Don't you try running off again. You do and Stick'll cut you up in little chunks!" he whispered. Gino's eyes looked like holes burnt in oilcloth.

They followed a path which ran along the stone wall, James and Gladys walking in front, the others wheeling their bikes, everyone silent.

After they'd walked a long time, Stick stopped. "We try this one," he said, looking up at the huge orange building which rose so high that James had to strain his neck to see the top of it. Blue found an exit from the park. Once more they were on the wide street. A little old man passed in front of them pushing a shopping cart. It was full of old newspapers. "Time is money," said the old man to himself.

James saw two doormen standing beneath the canopy of the building. Blue was giggling and shaking his head. "Look up there!" he said. "Those fools got trees growing on their porches!" James looked up and saw the tops of two good-sized trees sticking up over the balcony.

"We got to put the dog in the box now," said Stick.

"No!" James cried.

Gino took the leash from his hand and led Gladys back into the park.

"Take it easy," Blue said to James. "That box is better than a nice bed. And it got holes in the top for air."

"All right," cut in Stick impatiently. "Now listen, Prince. You do the same thing you did last time. Tell them your mama is up there. Pick a high floor. Go!"

Hopelessly, James crossed the street. He was tired and hungry and his arms felt as if they hardly belonged to him. He didn't much care what happened now. He even wondered if it wouldn't be better if he got caught. Somebody might give him something to eat then.

He had no trouble at all. The doormen were deep in a conversation and barely noticed him. The lobby walls were covered with mirrors and James saw his reflection, walking to the elevator, pressing the button, disappearing. He had told the doormen his mother worked on the eighteenth floor but he was scared to go up that high so he pressed the button that said 10.

When the elevator door slid back, James found himself in a small hall with one large window taking up one wall. Opposite the elevator was a table standing on little thin legs. On the table was a bowl of dried flowers. There were only two doors. One was marked, "Service Entrance." He pressed the button next to the other. At once there was an explosion of barks, great deep woofs, snarling and growling. James backed into the window and turned to the elevator. But it was already sliding down, out of sight. There was no place to hide or to go.

The door opened silently. James cried out as an enormous brown dog, its mouth opened like a cave, reared up and snapped at the air. James crouched at the foot of the table. The bowl rolled off and the flowers scattered over the floor of the little hall. He covered his eyes with his hands. Then there was a sound that made James think the dog was laughing at him — it was such a dog-like laugh. He took his hands away from his face and looked up. The dog was still standing there but he was leashed with a metal chain held by a very fat man.

The man had on a dirty-looking black coat and a T-shirt like Aunt Grace wore when she cleaned out their room. On his head was a flat gray hat with uneven edges, all chewed up, looking as though the dog had gotten hold of it. The man stopped laughing, hiccupped, then started up again.

"How do you like that?" the man cried. "I got a dog like a mountain lion! He scared you, didn't he? Don't move!"

"I got off on the wrong floor," said James in a faint whisper, afraid to stir in any direction, afraid to speak out loud.

"You hear that, Rudy?" said the man to the dog. "This little man says he got off on the wrong floor! Shall we ask him to pick up those flowers like a nice little man? Eh, Rudy? What did you say?"

Rudy said nothing, but suddenly lay down. His huge head rested on his paws.

"Pick up the flowers, dear child," said the

man, his little mouth twitching with giggles. "And put them in the bowl, and put the bowl back exactly in the middle of the table."

James gathered up the flowers and stuck them back in the bowl. Some of them turned to dust as soon as he touched them.

"Now," said the fat man, "ring for the elevator and we'll find your floor for you."

"I got to go home now," said James. He fumbled for the elevator button.

As soon as the elevator door opened, James slid inside and crouched in a corner. The fat man followed, and Rudy slouched in last, taking long floppy steps. Then Rudy sat down. Sitting, he was as tall as James.

"I certainly hope you've learned your lesson," said the man.

What lesson? wondered James.

When they arrived at the main floor, James raced out and crossed the lobby, passed the two doormen, sped under the canopy and out onto the street, not even bothering to look for cars. Stick and Blue and Gino were all staring at something behind him. James ducked behind Blue, then peered around him. The fat man was walking sedately on the other side of the street.

"He didn't need anybody to take that dog for a walk," James gasped. Even Stick laughed.

"Look at that big ugly old thing," said Blue.

"Which one?" asked Gino.

Blue held out a paper bag to James. He opened it and found two sugar doughnuts inside.

"Do I have to go back in there?" James asked Stick.

Stick was looking down the columns of a newspaper. No one answered James.

"Whatchu looking in that paper for?" Gino asked. "Come on man . . . you can't read."

"See that!" Stick said, gesturing with his head at the page.

"I see where we can buy us a Rolls Royce for only $9,000," said Blue as he poked his head over Stick's shoulder.

"No, no . . ." Stick muttered. "Look down there where it say *sealyham.*"

"How about a Jaguar?" asked Blue.

"You looking at the pictures," Gino said, sneering. "Can't you even spell *reward,* Fat?"

"See it, Gino?" asked Stick. "They got the phone number there."

"Yeah," Gino answered. "Who's going to call the people this time?"

"He going to," Stick said, pointing at James.

"How much you think we're going to get," Blue asked, "if it's the right dog?"

"Maybe $10," said Stick. "That sealyham not worth more'n that."

James wanted to ask them what they were talking about. What was a sealyham? What phone call was he going to make? Telephones were *bad* news. He didn't like them.

"Do I have to — " he started to ask again.

"We change our plans. We're headed for Coney Island. Tomorrow you can get us another dog."

Tomorrow! The piece of doughnut in his mouth felt like glue. Tomorrow. They weren't going to let him go. Why had he ever thought that all of this would be over by tomorrow? Why had he thought that he would be back home in his own bed with the coat spread out over him and his own box of things beneath the bed? He'd never get away from them — Gino would see to that.

He dragged himself up on the back of Gino's bike. He wasn't hungry anymore. The paper bag was squashed between his chest and Gino's back. He could smell the sugar and the cinnamon and through that, the leathery smell of Gino's black jacket.

Where was Gladys?

He shouted at Blue who was riding alongside. "In the box. Sleeping," Blue shouted back.

Sleeping. James leaned against Gino's back. They were going at great speed now, through the park, down the long slopes, around curves. Coney Island. Where was that? He closed his eyes. He was more tired than he had ever been in his life. They were taking him farther and farther away from all the places he knew. He and Gladys. James fell asleep.

5

James awoke to find himself flying beneath a black sky. His cheek, pushed up against the leather of Gino's coat, was warm and damp. But when he moved his head, the air was icy. He heard a bumping sound as though something were being dragged over boards. There was a peculiar smell; it tickled his nose, and it was sharp and clear. Sometimes the smell was like wet wood. There was another sound, louder than the bumping, a sound like many people murmuring down a hall just far enough away so that he couldn't make out what was being said. He hoped Gladys was all right.

She was probably warmer than he was — at least she had fur.

They rode under a street lamp. Blue, riding next to Gino, cried, "Man, it's so cold out here. So cold. . . ." James strained to see where he was. The road they were riding on was made of wide black boards. Along it ran a fence made of iron pipes. By squinting, James could make out, below them, a white line which moved constantly. First it was far away, then it rushed forward, broke, and when it broke there came the sound of murmuring.

"What's that?" James called out to Blue.

"What's that?" echoed Blue, shaking his head. "Prince, you don't know nothing. *That* is the Atlantic Ocean."

Stick came up fast on the other side, his head down like a racer. "You swim straight across, Prince, and you'll get to Africa," he shouted.

"Simba!" yelled Blue. "Go, bwana, go!"

"Shut up!" Stick cried. "We almost there. You gonna wake up those Coney cops."

A shape rose up suddenly on their left, darker than the sky. Soaring up, dropping down, the empty track of a roller coaster seemed, on its narrow struts, about to topple over on the four of them. An immense Ferris wheel started up where the roller coaster ended like a giant loop at the end of a letter. Its cars were all locked into position, looking like beetles hanging there.

Ahead of them, James saw a cluster of lights, and at that moment a freezing wind sprang up. A faded poster rustled across the wooden boards, and by the light from a street lamp, James could see a picture of a huge fat woman in a sparkly dress sitting on a purple throne and, standing next to her, a dwarf, a real dwarf. They were slowing down, and James spelled out the words across the top of the poster, "House of Freaks." The three bicycles came to a halt.

"We got to go on the beach here, down where the sand is hard," said Stick. "That cop hangs around there where the lunchroom is."

"Yeah," said Gino, "stuffing his fat cop face."

"Oh, they got to eat," Blue said. "Makes them meaner when they doesn't eat."

Cold and miserable though he was, James felt dizzy with excitement. He wanted to get nearer that water with its strange smell. Blue headed down the stairs to the darkness below. James slid off the back of Gino's bike and took hold of the pipe railing. It was clammy, and as he ran his hand along it his fingers stuck as if they had glue on them.

"Don't bump the dog," he said to Gino who was lifting the bike down.

"Don't tell me nothing," said Gino nastily.

At the foot of the stairs James bent down and touched the sand. It was fine and damp, and he liked the feel of it. He grabbed up a handful and put it in his pocket. He trudged along behind the others, down toward the white line which was the foam from the breaking waves. The strange smell was very close now. The darkness was immense. It was like a thing, an animal, something filling up the night. The spokes of the bicycle wheels glinted in the light from the street lamps on the boardwalk. A very few stars gleamed far over the ocean. The water raced up the sloping sand. James felt it swirling around his feet. It was icy yet he didn't care. Gino grabbed his arm. "Come on, come on. . . ."

"Yeah, Prince," said Blue. "You got to practice before you can swim that ocean."

"No more talking," Stick ordered. "Not till we get past the lights."

The wheels rolled forward on the sand. Gino in his black jacket was nearly invisible except for his small pale face. Blue walked with his head down, his back bent over his bicycle. Stick kept his eyes turned toward where the cluster of lights lost their blurred sparkle and grew clear. James saw a few people wrapped in coats and huddled together as they leaned over the railing, facing out toward the ocean. Behind them were several squat buildings. One was a restaurant. James could see a boy wearing a cook's hat leaning on his elbow on a counter. Just behind him was a frankfurter grill. A policeman was talking to the boy. His hands were waving wildly. A fat woman detached herself from the group at the railing, pulled up her collar and began to walk over to the counter.

By the light of the lamps, James saw the color of the sand, grayish white. There were big green trash baskets everywhere on the beach. A bit of crumpled paper blew up against one and stuck to the wire.

As the four of them passed in the shadows, the fat woman turned. She held two hotdogs, one in each hand. Even from where he was, James could see the mustard. Was she the woman in the poster? From far away came the sound of a piano and someone singing. The voice whipped back and forth like a ribbon in the wind. James made out a few of the words:

> *There are smiles*
> *that make you h-a-a-appy. . . .*
> *There are smiles*
> *that make you blu-u-u-u-e. . . .*

James looked at Blue. But he could barely see him or the others. It was too dark.

"We can turn up here . . . get back on the boardwalk," whispered Stick. A large wave broke softly behind them like Stick's whisper magnified. The bicycles were pushed up a few cement steps. James turned back and looked straight out across the water, thinking of it rolling all the way to Africa and breaking into waves on another beach.

"Come on. Give it a push," said Gino. James put his frozen hands on the back fender and shoved. He dreaded getting back on the bicycle because his legs were so sore.

Holding onto Gino, the wheels turning faster and faster beneath them, James thought of his Aunts. It was night there too. What would his Aunts be thinking? All the people in the building would be crowded into the room saying, "Where is James? Oh, where, where is James?" The wind dried his tears as fast as they rolled down his cheeks.

Had his Aunts known about this ocean all along? Did everybody know about it? How could you get across it unless you had a boat? His mother could have gotten a boat. But how long would a boat take to cross? Looking out beyond the railing, there was no sky, only the water taking up all the space and going on to the end of everything. How could she have taken enough food to last her? Oh, he knew about those big ships that went back and forth. But you needed money to ride on them. Where would his mother get the money? When he asked her for a nickel, she used to dig around inside that little black change purse where she kept her wedding ring and some hairpins, hardly ever money, real money. As for her getting her own boat, no little rowboat could get all the way to the other beach on the other side. It was terrible to think of his mother out there in the black night bobbing around on the top of that water, by herself.

They stopped again, this time beside a large door which rose high above them. It was covered with tattered posters and signs, and it was open and creaking in the wind. They stood there shivering.

"Blue, ride back and buy hotdogs, as many as you can get for this," said Stick. He handed Blue a dollar and some change. The dollar was all crumpled up as though it had been in his pocket for a long time. "Get some coffee too."

"Why can't Gino go?" Blue asked.

"Because he's gonna stay," Stick said, his scowl visible in the darkness. Blue shrugged and turned his bike toward the restaurant.

"Come on," commanded Stick. "We got to take the bikes inside. That cop hasn't been here since we left last night."

"Where are we?" asked James softly.

"Whadda you care," growled Gino.

Gladys whimpered. "Get it out of the box," Stick said to James. He lifted the box lid. Gladys was all curled up on some rags. James lifted her out. She crept next to his feet and lay down. He bent down to scratch her head. Her ribbon had come untied and she didn't seem very lively.

"Put the leash on her," Stick said. James clipped the leash onto Gladys' collar. "Let's go," he said, pushing the big door back. Inside it was pitch black. As they walked on the wooden floor, there were echoes. Glady's nails clicked. It was a comforting sound. Gradually James could make out dim shapes of all sizes — they seemed to be hanging in the air or sticking up straight out of the floor.

"Where are we?" he asked again, not hoping for an answer. Blue was the only one who would really say anything to him. The air smelled like wet cardboard, but the ocean smell was there too, more powerful than anything else.

"This is a funhouse," said Stick. Gino laughed.

"Yeah," Stick continued. "Yeah, this is the place where all the people come in the summer. They kill themselves in here. There's everything to ride, wheels and little cars, and slides and all kinds of crazy things. Everybody laugh and everybody scream. That's what they call fun." His voice sounded strange, as if he were secretly laughing at the people who came to this place.

"And they got to pay for it," said Gino. "It cost plenty money."

"Turn," said Stick abruptly. James stumbled against a step. They went up a flight of stairs as long as the stairs in the house where James lived. Gladys was having a hard time. James bent down, picked her up and carried her the rest of the way.

"Let me go first," said Stick and pushed open a door. There was a low growl. Gino lit a match and, shielding it with his hand, stooped to the floor.

"Here it is," said Stick, kicking a candle over to Gino. After lighting it, Gino stuck it in an empty Coke bottle that was lying nearby.

The room was so small the three of them filled it up. The ceiling was so low that Stick had to keep his head bent. A broken chair stood in a corner on three legs. Down on the floor, their leashes tied together, were two small dogs. Gladys strained so to get out of James' arms that he let her go. She leaped to the other dogs. They wagged their tails and sniffed each other.

"Look at that," said Stick. "They still here."

"What'd you think they was going to do? Take

the subway home?" asked Gino.

"You got the dog food?" asked Stick.

"Yeah, I got it," answered Gino.

"And the can-opener?"

"Yeah," said Gino.

"Now listen," Stick said, tapping James on the shoulder, "we're going to take the dogs out to the beach for a few minutes. Don't you leave this room! Now — pay attention to me! You try running down those stairs, you'll fall into the biggest, blackest hole there is. You hear? There's traps down there and there's *other things* too bad for me to tell you!"

They were going to leave him alone! It might be his chance. The thought that he could get away made him forget his fear of being by himself in the room, even made what Stick said unimportant, like something written in chalk on the sidewalk.

After they had gone, taking the three dogs with them, James listened at the door until he could no longer hear their footsteps or the bumping sound the dogs made going down the stairs. The little candle burnt steadily. If he followed Stick and Gino down the stairs, he might run into Blue. Maybe he wasn't one of those "other things" Stick talked about, but Blue was bad enough. How else could he get out? There wasn't a window in the room. Then James saw, just behind the chair, a break in the smoothness of the wall surface and just above it a very small sign that said THIS WAY OUT. Someone had written across it, in red crayon, "ha-ha." As he drew closer, he realized it was a small door but not an ordinary one. It had no handle and no knob. He pushed at it with his hand. It swung back instantly. He held up the candle. Above he could make out arched steel girders. Below, the floor was shiny yellow as though it had been recently painted, and it sloped slightly. But directly in front of him, the candle threw no light.

He backed away from the door. He listened. Was there anything stirring out there? The candle flame flickered and shrank. If it went out and he had to wait in the dark for Gino and Stick, it would be almost as awful as having to walk through that door in the dark. A violent little splutter of burning wax crackled next to his ear, and the candle light died. James dropped it on the floor and flung himself through the hole in the wall.

Almost at once his legs shot out from under him. He was in total darkness, falling. Yet he could feel the smooth surface of wood on which he slid and circled and turned and rolled. He clenched his jaws to keep from crying out. All at once he came to a stop. He closed his eyes to shut out the dizziness. He was afraid to move, afraid to stay where he was, flat on his back. His hands burned and the seat of his pants was warm as though he'd been sitting on a radiator. Was he on the edge of something? Was it safe to sit up? He opened his eyes. Everything was still. He got slowly to his feet, remembering this was the way he had stood when he was very small — first putting his hands on the floor, then wobbling his way up until he was standing.

It was hard to see anything. The darkness had a kind of soft hum that made him feel breathless. Gradually he was able to make out the odd-looking shapes of the things in the vast room. Behind him was the enormous slide down which he had just fallen. He knew now why someone had written "ha-ha" above the little door. A few feet in front of him something was hanging at the level of his forehead. He took a few steps and reached up, his hand grazing a thick wooden board. He clutched it. A chain clanked. It belonged to a swing suspended from a center pole. He heard a bark. Grabbing the seat with both hands, he hoisted himself up. It was so like a playground swing that for a second James imagined himself staring down at the cement, hearing the shouts of the children on other swings.

He felt himself turning slowly, the chain tangling above him. But he couldn't reach the floor to steady the swing. He just hoped no one walked near him.

"Hurry!" someone said.

"I can't see nothin'!"

"You don't have to see nothin'! Just move!"

It was Stick and Gino. James drew his feet up onto the swing, crouching.

"Why can't we light a match?" asked Gino.

"How do you know what's walking around in here?" Stick asked. They were so close now that James could see them, their shoulders about level with the edge of the swing. One of the dogs growled. Stick and Gino stood still.

"Somebody's in here . . ." Gino whispered.

"You crazy," Stick said.

"Then maybe *something* is in here," Gino said. "Maybe it ain't alive."

"Something like *you*," Stick muttered. "Come on, now. We got a lot to do."

"I don't like this place," Gino said.

"Come *on*!" Stick urged.

One of the dogs whimpered.

"What's the matter with it?" asked Gino.

"Now, how would I know that?"

"Look. It's sitting down!" Gino cried.

"Then drag it," Stick said angrily.

It must be Gladys, thought James. She knows I'm here.

"It's standing up on its hind legs. . . ." Gino sounded scared. "You know I don't like to touch them."

"Pick up that dog and carry it," Stick ordered. "Let's get upstairs where we can get the candle."

"Okay, okay. . . ."

A blur of light way up near the ceiling spilled into the darkness like pale yellow paint. James could see Gino and Stick standing in front of the little room at the top of the stairs. The swing swayed gently, turned ever so gently on its chains like a branch in a breeze. For a second he lost sight of them, then the swing untwisted itself and he saw Gino drop Gladys on the floor and go into the room.

"He's gone!" Gino shouted.

Stick ran in after him. From another direction, James heard someone whistling and the sound of a bicycle being rolled over the floor. Blue started up the stairs. James smelled mustard and leaned out of the swing, sniffing hungrily.

The three appeared again at the top of the stairs, Gino holding the candle high. They were whispering. Blue looked back down the stairs. Gino laughed suddenly. The sound of it was like a little knife cutting through the thick dark all around James, tearing it open so he was there for everyone to see. Gladys stood next to Blue, her tail wagging feebly. James felt terrible about Gladys at that moment. She must be frightened and homesick. He had never had anything to do with a dog before, yet sitting there as if he was on some ordinary playground swing instead of in this crazy funhouse in the middle of the night, he felt he cared more about Gladys than anything in the world — except his mother. The thought of his mother surprised him. He hadn't had a picture of her in his mind for a while. Well, she couldn't help him now. He was completely alone.

Gladys was hopping down the stairs and just behind her, his head bent forward intently, was Stick. Gladys stopped. Stick waited. She'd give him away! James stopped feeling sorry for her. Gladys dropped down some more steps, Stick close to her. Then James lost sight of them but he could still hear the dog. Now she was running from place to place, whimpering and barking. Stick's sneakers thumped on the wood floor. For a second there was no sound at all. Then he heard Gladys panting. They were near enough so he could have reached out and touched Stick. Gladys yipped excitedly. James gripped the chains of the swing. At that same moment, the swing stopped moving; the chains were rigid. James let go and hid his face in his hands. He had been found.

"Bring down the candle," shouted Stick. James peered through his fingers. As Blue drew near the bottom, the flickering light revealed more of the huge room. James saw the slide. He saw wooden tunnels big enough for people to walk through, a long wall of mirrors, a stack of little open cars, each one big enough for a person to sit in, and way over near the back of the room, a row of painted horses on a track.

"Look at that!" exclaimed Blue.

James took his hands from his face and stared down at Stick's eyes. Stick's head was right at the level of his knees. James groaned and slumped in the swing.

"You trying out the amusements?" Blue asked, holding the candle so close to James' feet that he could feel the heat. "Why, these are closed now, sir. Closed for the winter. Nothing in here except ghosts. . . ."

"Get down from there," Stick ordered. "Get off that thing, Prince."

"Hey. I'm up here by myself," came Gino's thin cry from above. "Bring back the light!"

At the sound of Gino's voice, James straightened up and leaped between Stick and Blue. His feet hit the floor with a painful thump. He ran toward the horses. Gladys was tangled in his legs. How he hated her at that moment! He ducked under a wooden turnstile, climbed over a low fence and found himself on a narrow metal track. Just ahead of him were the painted horses. Suddenly the light went out. He heard Stick and Blue swearing, and Gino howling above. The candle must have fallen on the floor. Gladys licked his hands. If only she'd be quiet, or follow somebody else! A match was struck; the light came back.

"Oh, Gladys, you'll give me away," whispered James. Just in back of him, the track on which he was standing rose high in the air. Ahead of him were the horses. They were mounted on little rollerskate wheels which fitted over the narrow rails of the track. He ran forward hoping he could hide beneath the horses' legs. When he reached the end horse, he ducked down and began to crawl, Gladys right beside him. He heard Blue and Stick running across the floor, and Gino whining. James kept going between the metal legs, scraping his ankles on the track and bumping into the horses. Then he came to the last horse.

But instead of a blank wall, he found an opening covered with a grille of thin wire. James grabbed hold of the wire and looked out. There, a few feet below, was the beach. There was the ocean, and the sky lit by a few faint stars. He sighed deeply. A wave broke like a giant echo of his sigh. Then he slid down, his back against the grille. Gladys crawled into his lap. He couldn't escape.

Looking down to the end of the tunnel formed by the horses' legs, he saw Blue crouching, the candle in his hand.

"Come on," Blue called. James pushed Gladys off his lap and began the long crawl to the light.

When they got back, up to the little room, Gino was standing there mumbling to himself, his hair sticking up like porcupine quills. He glared fiercely at James.

"I ought to break your head," he said.

"That's two," Stick said to James. "You try one more time — and you're *out.*"

"Leave him be," Blue said. "We're gonna get plenty use out of him."

"Get in there and feed those dogs," Stick ordered James, as he clipped on the dogs' leashes.

James opened the cans, dug out the dog food with the handle of the can-opener and set out three little heaps on the newspaper.

"You gonna give them the aspirin now?" Blue asked Stick.

"No," said Stick. "We give it to them now, it'll wear off before we get back to the house."

Gladys took little bites as if she didn't care much for the food, but the other two dogs gulped it down in a minute.

Blue handed James a hotdog covered with mustard and catchup and relish. James was too hungry to taste it — he just swallowed.

"Get out that newspaper, Blue," Stick said. "I want to figure out when to call those people about the sealyham."

"Call them now," Gino said. "We get the money " —he smacked one fist into the palm of the other hand —"and then we divide it up."

"Yeah," Stick said. "You build me a phone right here and I'll call the people in the middle of the night and then you take the dog back and after that, Blue and me, we'll come and visit you in jail."

"What's that?" James whispered to Blue. "A sealyham?"

"You don't know about dogs, do you, Prince," Blue said. "We know. We experts. These are special dogs. They got their own beds and their own winter coats. They even got raincoats. They go to special places to get their beauty treatment, see? You just seen those old mutts out in the street. They are *nothing* dogs. But these dogs here, they like you, Prince. They special. *Royal!*"

"You got a big mouth," Gino said, looking over the edge of the newspaper Stick was reading.

"And you got no mouth," Blue said angrily. "You just got that mean little line there in the middle of your mean little face."

"I'll kick you both downstairs," Stick said very softly.

Blue's mouth moved violently but he said nothing. Suddenly Stick froze. Gino blew out the candle. James felt Stick's hand wrap itself around his arm. Were they going to kill him in the dark?

"Somebody coming," muttered Blue, and they all moved to the door, Stick dragging James by his arm.

There was no sound except for the soft, restless padding of the dogs as the three animals circled at the ends of their leashes.

At first, James heard only a thin tuneless whistle, then a kind of thump like a stick banging on a door. The whistle turned into humming. It was the kind of singing noise James had heard people make when they were walking down the street and had forgotten where they were.

Far below, the door leading to the boardwalk was flung back. The beam of a flashlight poked into the huge room and snaked its way from tunnel to slide to mirror, across the floor and back, up and down. As the beam crossed the line of mirrors, the reflection of a policeman flashed for an instant into full view. James could see his cap and badge and the black stick he held in one hand.

What if he tried to yell? But James felt he had no more air in him, that if he didn't breathe soon his throat would close up. What if he could yell? What would Stick or Gino, even Blue, do to him before the policeman could get up those stairs?

The flashlight clicked off. Grabbing the door, the policeman pulled it shut. James heard a hard metal click.

Gino lit a match and lit the candle. Then he and Blue raced down the stairs. Their shadows sprang upon the walls and mirrors like the shadows of giants. Blue took hold of the door and yanked.

"He's padlocked the door on the outside," Gino called back to Stick. "We're stuck!"

"Locked in the funhouse," Blue cried.

"Fool!" grunted Stick. "Hold these dogs, Prince."

James waited at the top of the stairs. The sealyham sat down on his foot. Gladys licked his hand. The spaniel moaned softly to itself like an old lady. He watched the three boys darting around the room looking for a place to get out. In the light from the candle, around which Gino's claw-like hand curved to protect the flame, they looked as though they were skating.

"Now what?" James heard Gino ask.

"We'll burn the place down," Stick cried furiously.

6

James' heart beat faster. Fire was the worst thing of all. He had seen fires, seen flaming mattresses hurled from windows, piles of charred sticks, baby carriages burned down to metal rims, heard people crying out, people wrapped in blankets, staggering, dazed, miserable.

"No!" Gino cried. "No fires!"

"What else?" asked Stick.

"There's a way out," James cried. The three faces turned up toward him. "An opening behind those horses," he said. "It's got something over it like fence wire. But we could maybe get it off."

"Come down here," Stick commanded.

James and the three dogs came down the stairs.

"Show me," said Stick.

James led him over to the painted horses. He stooped down. "Bring that candle to me," Stick said to Gino. James pointed along the track. "It's down there," he said. Stick climbed over the fence and onto the track but he couldn't squeeze beneath the horses.

"You'll have to do it," he told James. "You and Gino. Come on, Gino. You a runt."

"How are we going to get the wire off the hole?" asked Gino.

Stick didn't answer him. Holding the candle high, he went off to search.

When he came back, he held a short length of pipe in one hand. "Here," he said. "Take it, Gino."

James led the way, creeping on his knees. Gino was right behind him, holding the candle. The flame flickered in the breeze that blew up from the beach.

While Gino worked on the wire, James held the candle. Gino worked quickly, prying and bending until, with a screech, one of the clamps that held the wire gave way, then another, until at last the opening was clear. Sweat stood out on

Gino's forehead; his mouth had disappeared altogether. He poked his head out, then withdrew it.

"There's about a four-foot drop to the sand," he called back to Stick.

"Get back here," Stick said.

They crawled down the track.

"Now, how are we gonna get the bikes underneath the horses?" asked Blue.

Stick frowned. Gino blew on his scraped knuckles. Blue shook his head slowly from side to side. "They'll never fit," he said.

"They'll fit or the place burns," Stick grunted.

"We could push the horses back," said James suddenly. "I felt one move a little when I went under it. They're just standing there on those rails."

Stick grunted, "The prince got a brain or two. More than either of you got." He went to the end horse, put his arm around its neck and pulled. Slowly, the horse moved back, noiseless on its track.

"Get those hosses into the corral!" Blue shouted in a cowboy accent.

"Get yourself over here and shove," said Stick.

James watched as the three of them pushed the horses back until there was enough space in front of the opening for a bicycle.

"You take care of the dogs till we start riding," Stick said to James.

It took three of them to lower each bike to the beach. James handed the dogs down to Blue. Then he jumped, landing on the moist cold sand. The funhouse, dark and shapeless, towered above them; the opening they had come through was as black as a pocket.

James felt almost hopeful, smelling the water, listening to the sound of the waves breaking.

"What'd you say the name of that was?" he asked Gino who was trudging ahead of him pushing the bike.

"I didn't say the name of anything," Gino said.

"The At-lan-tic," said Stick very clearly as though he were about to spell the word. "The At-lan-tic Ocean."

Once they were back on the boardwalk, Stick ordered them to load up the dogs.

"Okay, Captain," said Blue. He picked up the sealyham, which grunted as Blue dropped it into the box on Stick's bicycle, then the spaniel, which looked sadly at James as it was placed in the box on Blue's bike. James got to Gladys first. He held her gently, then put her into Gino's box. Her ribbon had come undone again. He tied it while Gino creaked and laughed. Blue said, "Now ain't that sweet? My! My! Wish I was a

nice little old dog with a nice little prince for a
mama!"

They rode fast, the boards rattling beneath
the wheels. The lights glistened on the empty
boardwalk, on the closed windows of the restaurant, on the dark shut-up buildings. It looked
lonely. There was only the sound of the waves,
and the wheels rolling.

"The Atlantic Ocean," James whispered to
himself, his face once more pushed against
Gino's jacket, his arms around Gino's middle.

The cold, the sudden shifts of direction, the
bicycles wheeling and swerving, the dark empty streets occasionally lit by a tall street lamp,
all seemed to James like the beginning of a
dream. The dream was without people, the only
living thing in it was the smell of the ocean,
sharp and sweet but especially new. It was a
new smell that belonged entirely to him, not
breathed by any other person alive. But the
smell began to fade. Soon there was nothing left
of it, its place taken by the old street smells he
knew. Then a few automobiles appeared, more
lights, a store or two. The street they were riding
on looked familiar. On one side were tall apartment houses; on the other a park.

Was this around where he had gotten Gladys?
James wondered. He looked at one of the big

buildings across the street. The glass doors were closed but he could see a doorman inside, leaning against a wall, his hat on the back of his head. He was suddenly sure that it was Gladys' building. He could see the number on it, 333. If James could only get away from them a minute, he could run to the doorman and hand Gladys over. He smiled, imagining how the lady would look when she saw the dog. She'd never know that Gladys had been all the way to the Atlantic Ocean. She wouldn't know *what* had happened to Gladys. But he couldn't get away. Not now. Usually, when things were hard for James, he could remind himself that in the morning he'd have a new chance, a fresh day. But this time, he didn't want to think about tomorrow. He couldn't believe there would *be* a tomorrow.

He thought he must be near home now because of all the people. No one seemed to sleep in his neighborhood. People were walking up and down the sidewalks, talking or whistling, or else standing in groups at the corners, their hands in their pockets. No one even bothered to look at the four of them as they rode on. James tried to decide whether he would rather be warm or full of supper. It seemed to him there was nothing more in the world to want at that moment than a warm bed, a glass of milk or a piece of toast covered with honey. He wondere~ Did Blue or Stick or Gino have beds somewhere? They couldn't be out on these bikes all the time — riding, riding, riding.

He didn't really recognize the streets. But they felt like home. Aunt Paul had taken him to a late movie once. She'd waked him up in the middle of the night and told him to get dressed. He had been frightened because she had sounded so strange and distant. That was the night his mother had gotten sick and had cried so much, sitting in a corner on the floor by herself, and letting the tears run down her face without drying them. By the time he and Aunt Paul got home from the movie, his mother had been taken to the hospital. That's what Aunt Grace had said. She said the doctors would take care of his mother and she'd be home soon. But the months passed. He hadn't remembered that night in a long time. He leaned against his own thoughts as though he were leaning against a door to keep it shut until the memory went away.

"Hold on!" shouted Gino as they went around a corner. They raced down the middle of an empty street. There were no people here, just a few parked cars. Stick slowed down. It was the street of the house and it looked as deserted now it did during the day. It was hard for James to believe the house was still there. He felt he had left it a hundred years ago.

They parked the bicycles around the side of the house and lifted the dogs out, clipped on their leashes and dropped them to the ground. The dogs ran back and forth, whimpering and sniffing the dead bushes.

"Take a look and see if somebody out there," Stick told Gino.

"Not me," Gino said. "Blue, you go."

"I said, *you*," Stick said. Gino stumped off around the corner.

"Nobody," his voice called back a minute later.

They walked up the steps and into the house through the doorway.

"Blue, you go down to the cellar and get that candle. Gino cover up those windows with the rags over there. Prince, you see these little white pills? You going to open up another can of dog food and take out three little hunks. You put one of these aspirins in each hunk and give it to the dogs." He handed James a can of dog food, the can opener and three flat white tablets.

James squatted down on the floor and began to open the can.

"You all right, Prince," Stick said softly as

though he were afraid someone might overhear him. "You do fine."

James didn't say anything. He was afraid of Stick, afraid of the knife he knew was in Stick's pocket. Yet he liked what Stick had said to him.

"I can't see to put the pills in," he said.

"Wait for the candle," Stick replied.

When Blue arrived with the candle, James took it with the dog food and the aspirin to the corner near the staircase where the dogs had been tied up. But James didn't put the tablets in the hunks of food he took from the can. James didn't want the dogs to go to sleep; he wanted them awake. He slipped the tablets into his pocket quickly, leaning over so no one could see what he was doing. The dogs took the food from his hands — even Gladys gobbled it up this time.

James went back to Stick who placed the candle on the floor. Gino was already rolled up in a corner, his knees almost touching his chin. Blue was sitting with his back against the wall, staring into the candlelight. Then Stick leaned over and blew out the candle. James crawled over near Blue.

"I saw that big old cardboard Sandy Claus down there," Blue whispered. "Man, what were you *doing*, dancing around in front of that thing?"

James didn't want to talk about that. He had known all along it was just a big cardboard cut-out.

"Where do you live?" James asked.

"All around," said Blue.

"I live with my Aunts. There's junkies in my building. A man got killed in the alley back of my house."

Blue said, "Oh yeah . . . they everywhere . . . junkies."

"Are you?" asked James.

"No, not me. I got a brother, he sometimes takes a little something. Then he go to sleep and he lay around the bed and nobody can move he take up so much room."

"Does Stick have another name?"

"Oh yeah," said Blue. "He's got another name. He'd cut my throat if I told you. You couldn't beat it out of him. What's your name, Prince?"

James didn't answer. He didn't want to tell Blue his name. "You go to school?" he asked Blue finally.

Blue laughed softly. "School? Now why would I want to do that for? I can read the street signs *now*. They're not going to show me how to read them any better."

"You both gonna sleep on the sidewalk if you don't shut up," Stick said from across the room.

One of the dogs stretched and yawned and lay down with a thump. Gino was snoring. There was a cold dusty smell in the room.

"You got another name, Blue?" asked James, keeping his voice low.

"Yeah. I got a whole bunch of names. But I picked my own."

"Where do you sleep? Don't you have a place to go home?"

"I sleep *wherever*," Blue answered. "I don't know where my people got to — and I wouldn't go to find them anyhow. What I like is a place where I be by myself. We all like that. See, Stick he see this old place and he say — look, that's our house! We ride by it day after day and we make sure nobody live here. Then we make our plan. This going to be our own place. Not only we got a house now but an office. Dog business incorporated. And anything else we want to do. We can pick up chairs on the street, and sometimes you can find a mattress somebody throw out. Stick, he already find a coffee pot in a pile of trash. I know it's going to work good. . . . But then we come in here and we find you!" Blue laughed softly. "We so *surprised.* Like we found a ghost that lived here, only it was no ghost. It was you, Prince! Come on. What's your real name?"

"Are you going to bring dogs here from now

on, instead of out there at Coney?" James asked.

"Yeah, yeah. Better here. There's a telephone down the street and this way we close to the customers."

Stick suddenly shouted. "Now, shut up!"

Gino moaned, "Lemme sleep. . . ."

James was sorry to have to stop talking with Blue. He hoped he would never see the three of them in daylight again but Blue hadn't been so bad to him.

He was sleepy himself but he must not fall asleep. He had to wait until he was sure they were all sleeping. Silently he took Blue's scarf from around his neck and folded his arms across his chest. He sat up straight, his back pressed so tightly against the wall he could feel little lumps of plaster. He opened his eyes wide and stared into the darkness in front of him, waiting.

7

It was a long wait until Blue's head sank down and Gino's snores came and went regularly. One of the dogs snored too. But Stick was not asleep.

As James' eyes grew accustomed to the dark, he could see Stick sitting up like a giant letter L. His head was turned away from James, but even so he felt Stick was thinking about him. It was almost as if they were speaking to each other in a mysterious way. Once he heard Stick sigh. It was a deep long sigh, the kind that Aunt Grace used to sigh in the evening when she sat down in her chair, her hands and fingers grasping the wooden arms as she lowered herself slowly to the old red pillow that covered the seat.

Blue grunted suddenly and slid all the way down to the floor. His heels scraped and thudded as he turned back and forth trying to find a comfortable spot. It was funny about Blue wanting to be by himself, James thought.

But how could you be by yourself? There was always someone breathing or snoring, talking or crying or humming. There was always someone fighting or moving furniture, or throwing it, or striking matches on the wall so that you could hear it all the way into the next room.

There were always bottles crashing on the pavement or someone walking up and down the stairs, bumping against things or playing a radio. Even on the street, people carried radios slung around their arms and the radios crackled like bacon frying in a pan. Car gears shifted or horns blew. Sirens screeched and wailed and police cars moaned. There was always water leaking somewhere . . . drip, drip, drip . . . or someone shouting or screaming or laughing, ha-ha-ha-HA!

The one place where James had ever been by himself was downstairs in the cellar of this old house. The only sounds there had been his own breathing, his own footsteps. But he wasn't so

sure he really wanted to be by himself the way
Blue did. Sometimes, waking up at night and
listening to his Aunts breathing, listening to the
beds creaking, he got scared. What if his Aunts
were turning into furniture? And the furniture
turning into something living?

"You awake?" whispered Stick.

"Yes," said James.

"You hungry?"

"Yes."

Stick chuckled. "Yeah, I know," he said. "But
you ought to do like me. See, I think of one thing,
like a hammer, or rain, or a street I know. I
think so hard I stop being hungry. Only thing
is — then I don't sleep. But if I do sleep, I get
hungry."

"Don't you eat anything?" asked James.

"Oh yeah. I eat. A lot sometimes. But the food,
it stick up in me like lumps." Stick paused and
when he spoke again, the sound of his voice had
changed. He sounded as if he hated James.

"Don't you sit up there all night like some old
man hiding there in the dark watching me!" he
said. He turned his head away. James heard
him mutter, "Gino, I'm going to break your
head if you don't stop all that noise!"

Gino mumbled something, but a minute later
he was snoring again. James' back ached, his

legs ached, his head felt funny. He didn't dare move for fear he would attract Stick's attention. The more he told himself to sit still, the more he twitched. Perhaps if he tried Stick's way of concentrating on something — but he couldn't. It was too much like being in school. Miss Meadowsweet had once told him that he didn't know *how* to listen, and that he wouldn't be able to find his way out of a paper bag if he kept on the way he was going. Was there something wrong with his hearing? she had yelled.

While Miss Meadowsweet had been yelling, James had been imagining himself inside a paper bag, an enormous brown paper bag with the top tied around with a piece of string. He felt as if he were in one now. Wasn't there any air in this room? Yet it was so cold.

He supposed Stick didn't go to school either. Why did *he* have to go? There was no point asking himself that question. He knew why. His Aunts made him go. His Aunt Grace told him how proud his mother would be when she came back from the hospital and saw all the good marks he was going to get someday, and heard the teachers say what a fine boy he was. But his mother — she had been sitting on the floor in a corner, crying. She wasn't proud, just sick.

He felt so bad, thinking about his mother

being sick, not strong and well, that he forgot where he was. And no matter what he pretended, he knew she couldn't have gotten across the Atlantic Ocean. He had *seen* that water: huge, filling up the sky, moving like an animal, gleaming where the starlight touched it.

Suddenly, James grew aware of a new sound in the room. He bent forward, listening. It was Stick. He had fallen asleep at last. James knew how people sounded when they slept. Straining his eyes, he could see that Stick's head had fallen forward on his chest. He guessed that Stick's trick of thinking hard about something hadn't worked. Maybe Stick had just been talking the way people did sometimes, boasting.

Slowly, James got up on his knees. No sound, no one stirred. He bent forward and began to creep over toward the dogs. One of them wagged its tail; it thumped and brushed against the floor. James halted. Blue turned restlessly. Gino had stopped snoring but his breathing was deep and easy. Stick looked like a statue.

James crept on. He reached forward, felt in the air and closed his hand gently around a dog's muzzle. Another of the dogs stood up and shook itself. James froze.

"What are you doing?" whispered Stick.

"I'm cold," James whispered back quickly.

"I'm getting nearer the dogs to keep warm." Stick grunted. His head sank forward slowly. James sat back on his heels, then let himself down silently. Gladys climbed into his lap and licked his face. He scratched her head, feeling the little bow still tied. Dogs made as much noise as people when they were sleepy, thumping and scratching and sighing. A long time passed. Hours, thought James.

When he was sure Stick was asleep again, he reached through the darkness, touching and grasping until he found the post to which the three leashes had been tied. It was hard to untie them. He would get one knot untied, then have to stop because he couldn't help making a little noise. Meanwhile the dogs were moving around, shaking themselves, wagging their tails. The spaniel put its paws on his shoulders and its nose in his ear. He didn't want the dogs to make noise now, or to move fast. But soon, he would want them to make all the noise they could. He would want them to run off in all directions. Especially that sealyham. It had money riding on it.

When he had the leashes in his hand at last, he had to wait again. The hardest part was coming. He glanced at the front door. Blue had tried to shut it earlier. Because of the broken hinges, it hadn't budged. A little light fell in a thin ray across the floor. James lay down among the dogs and slowly began to wriggle toward the door. If he could stay in that position, he might make it, even though he'd have to stand up when he got to the door. Sometimes he moved easily and sometimes he didn't seem to move more than an inch or two. The dogs were getting lively. They were stepping all over him now. But he couldn't wait. He knew there wouldn't be another chance.

He was halfway across now. It seemed to him that he was making a tremendous racket. Perhaps it was only the loudness of his heart beating. In the light from the doorway, he could see the dogs quite clearly now. They were straining forward, their noses pointed at the door. The sealyham lifted its front paw. Gladys turned her head to look down at him. The spaniel's tail wagged slowly.

Now, he told himself. He got to his feet in a rush, the dogs clambering against his legs. He and the dogs together rushed at the door. Pushing against it, feeling it stand there like a rock, edging around it, seemed to take five minutes. The dogs were leaping in their eagerness to get out.

Then they were out. He took the steps with

one jump, jerking the leashes forward, landing on the sidewalk with a mighty smack of his shoes and racing to the street. Then he dropped the leashes. The spaniel barked, the sealyham answered and Gladys yipped. James turned only once to look back as he ran down the middle of the dark empty street. Gino was just coming out of the door. Behind him staggered Blue, rubbing his eyes. James didn't wait to see if Stick was coming.

All three dogs were barking wildly now as James' feet hit the pavement, lifted, stretched, hit again. He had never run so fast in his life. There wasn't enough breath left in him to shout. Around the corner he careened into another empty street. Gladys was still with him, tangled between his legs. He couldn't stop to push her away, couldn't do anything but run!

Turning another corner, James found himself on a broad avenue full of cars and lighted stores and people moving on the sidewalks. He slipped among a crowd of women all dressed up in fancy hats. They were all talking to each other and hardly noticed him at first. He slowed down to walk, gasping for breath.

"Why, look at that cute little dog! Is that your little dog?" A lady in a bright red coat stooped over next to him and patted Gladys. She stood up on her hind legs like a little circus dog and all the ladies formed a circle around her and James. He picked up her leash.

"We got to go," he said to the lady in the red coat who was smiling at him.

"Look at that ribbon," said another lady.

"I got to take her home," said James. The ladies made way for him just as the light turned red and the cars stopped. James looked across the avenue and saw Gino on the opposite sidewalk. James stayed where he was, among the ladies. All of them, Gladys and he in the middle, moved on down the avenue. They came within a few feet of an alleyway that separated a vegetable store and a pawnshop. He knew that pawnshop; he wasn't far from home now. He pushed his way through the group of ladies who were all murmuring among themselves like pigeons, and he and Gladys sped down the alley into an empty lot.

On the street side, there were some old wooden doors lined up to make a fence but there was an opening between two of them. The ground was rough. When the building that had been there was torn down, all the bricks and stones and boards had been left lying around. There were broken bottles and rusty beer cans everywhere. James scraped his ankles and his knees but Gladys ran lightly over everything. They emerged from between the two wooden doors upon another sidewalk. There were fewer people here and no stores. James felt almost safe. He knew Gino hadn't spotted him. He might not even know about the alley and how it went from the avenue to this street. James hoped the others were still chasing the spaniel and the sealyham.

But what was he going to do with Gladys? She was sitting at his feet looking up at him.

"Go home, Gladys," James said, "so I can go home."

She didn't move.

He couldn't take her back to his room. Aunt Grace said dogs were dirty things. Besides, they all would want to know where he had found her. *Found* her! He had stolen her! As it was, he didn't know what he was going to tell them.

"Oh, Gladys," he said. "How am I going to get you back?" He began to walk down the street, thinking. No one paid any attention to him now. But he wasn't surprised. The only things most people ever looked at around here were fires or fights.

He was stiff and sore. Along with the pain in his head, his right leg hurt. He would have to take her back.

"Come on, Gladys," he said. "You're going home."

There was no use in thinking about all the walking he had to do. Aunt Grace said you had to choose: Think about something or do it — a person couldn't do both. Aunt Paul said you could do both but it was harder. Meanwhile, he was walking, putting down one foot, then the other. It wasn't going to be too hard to find Gladys' building. James knew where the park was. Once he found that, he could find the street. He wondered what was making him move. And no story could make the distance pass quicker. Too much had happened — it all got in the way of each story he tried to begin.

He saw the trees of the park rising on the other side of another big avenue. He crossed over, keeping to the sidewalk which paralleled the park, followed it around a corner and found himself on the long, long street with the big buildings, Gladys' street. Just walk, he told himself. Gladys whimpered and jumped up against his legs. "I can't carry you," James said.

From time to time, he glanced at the buildings across the street. He didn't look at each one because it made his neck too tired. There were hardly any lights on. It must be pretty late, James thought — almost morning. Gladys pulled hard on the leash. She was trying to head toward the street. There was number 333. He heard the click of a traffic light changing. Only one car shifted its gears and drove on.

James halted a few feet away from the building entrance. He could just see into the lobby. The doorman was slumped in a green chair, his hat pulled down over his forehead. His hands were clasped in his lap and his coat came almost to his ankles.

What if this isn't the right building? thought James. It certainly wasn't the right doorman. Well, he couldn't stand there the rest of the night trying to make up his mind. Gladys was whimpering again. He moved forward quickly and leaned against the door. It opened silently. Silently, he bent down and patted Gladys. Then he let her go. The doorman slept on, but not for long.

Gladys flung herself at his feet. The doorman jumped up, and his hat fell off. Gladys raced back and forth, barking. The doorman leaned over, scooped her up and walked over to the panel where all the buttons were. He pressed one and picked up the telephone. James didn't wait any longer. It was all right, he thought, as he walked back across the street to the park side.

"Hey, you!" a voice shouted. James glanced behind him. The doorman was standing at the door clutching Gladys under one arm and waving with the other. James ran without looking back.

When he felt a safe distance away, he slowed down to a walk, then he stopped altogether and looked longingly at a wooden bench backed up against the stone wall. It would be nice to sit down for a few minutes. He started toward the bench, stopped. What he had thought was a bundle of rags and newspapers moved and groaned. James stared. A man was lying there resting his head on his hands which were pressed together beneath his cheek as though he were praying. One foot had slipped over the edge of the bench. The shoe had no laces; the tongue hung out lopsided.

Suddenly the man rose up, scattering rags and newspapers all around himself. His eyes were barely open.

"You got a nickel?" he cried hoarsely. "You got a cigarette? You got something for me?"

Once more, James ran. He couldn't manage a burst of speed. He was running in slow motion. When he stopped to look back, the man had fallen on the bench, a heap of rags again.

The traffic lights looked pale. They sky was

the color of garbage cans. It was almost dawn. Hardly any cars went by. James passed an old woman wearing sneakers and speaking rapidly to herself. He passed a cat slinking alongside of the stone wall.

Papers rustled in the gutters. He came to the avenue that marked the end of the park. There were more people now, all wrapped up in scarves and coats. He passed three men who were talking in loud voices to each other. One had a bandaged leg, one had a bandaged arm, the third had a bandaged head. A man came out of a store entrance and began to push back the heavy metal grille which had covered the glass of the store windows.

He had come to his own street. He turned down it. More cars, more people. He saw a yellow dog sniffing at a garbage can. He had given up thinking of what to tell his Aunts. No story was good enough. He would have to tell them what had really happened.

Then he was there, in front of the brown door with the broken window in it. Just inside a woman dozed in a straight chair. There was hardly enough room to get by her. It was Aunt Paul.

James opened the door. Aunt Paul opened her eyes. She looked at James for a long time without speaking, then she took his arm and pulled him toward her.

"We thought you was dead," she said. "We thought you was killed."

Aunt Grace came down the narrow hall. Her arms were crossed. Her hair was pulled up tight into a knot at the back of her head.

"We had the police," she said.

From behind her, Aunt Althea spoke. "We had a detective," she said.

Aunt Paul stood up, holding onto James. "He's back!" she cried.

James heard doors opening all over the building. People called out to each other, repeating over and over again, *"He's back, he's back!"*

"Your Aunt Paul was sick, she was so upset," said Aunt Grace.

"We was all sick," said Aunt Althea.

"Miss Meadowsweet came," said Aunt Paul. "She cried. She said you was a nice boy."

"I ought to smack you good!" Aunt Grace said, then burst into tears.

"They wouldn't let me go," said James as loud as he could. He looked up the stairwell where all the people were, dressed in their nightclothes, leaning over the railing, looking down. "They made me ride for miles. I went to Coney. I saw the Atlantic Ocean. They stole dogs. Listen, all of you, they kept watch on me. But I got away even though there was three of them."

"Hush!" said Aunt Grace, wiping her cheeks. "You got to come upstairs. You tell us later. I have to call the police station. Althea, give me ten cents."

Aunt Paul took James' hand in her own as Aunt Althea poked around in the pockets of her jacket. She handed a dime to Aunt Grace who went down the hall to where the public telephone hung on the wall.

"Come along," said Aunt Paul.

They went up. All the people who had been hanging over the stairs looked at James as though they couldn't believe what they saw. Some of the women patted his head as he went by and murmured again, "He's back. Look! He came back!"

James leaned against Aunt Paul as they stood in front of the familiar door. She pushed him ahead of her.

"I'm hungry," James said as he walked into the room. He looked at the table which had a red cloth on it, with a little can of evaporated milk sitting in the middle. He looked at the big bed where Aunt Grace and Aunt Althea slept. He looked at Aunt Paul's bed. The beds hadn't been slept in. He looked at the linoleum floor, at the hole in the ceiling, at the coffee pot. Then he looked at his bed.

A small woman was sitting on it. Her hair was cut close to her head so that it looked like one of the thistledowns Miss Meadowsweet had brought to school for nature study. She had on a dark dress and she was wearing slippers. She was hardly any bigger than Gino.

James stood still. But where were her long white robes? Her long black hair? Where were her servants and her crown?

Aunt Paul pushed him forward. He took a step. Why, she was hardly any bigger than he was! How *could* she be his mother?

He was so tired. He wanted to lie down somewhere, anywhere. He couldn't move. Then James felt happy. He would not have to go back to that old house. He would not have to walk down those cellar steps or see that giant cardboard figure anymore. He felt in his pocket for the ring. Then he remembered where the ring was. When he brought out his hand, it was coated with fine sand.

He thought, who am I? I'm not a prince. How can I be a prince? Who am I?

As though she had read his mind and heard his question, his mother held out her hand.

"Hello, Jimmy," she said.